MW01132790

Hill House

A Harry Starke Novel
By
Blair Howard

HILL HOUSE

A Harry Starke Novel

ISBN-13: 978-1519795779

Acknowledgements:

I would like to thank Jerry Redman of Second Life of Chattanooga for his help and expertise. Jerry is leading the fight to eliminate sex trafficking in Greater Chattanooga and Southeast Tennessee.

Chapter 1

It was going to be one of those weeks. I was sure of it. Heather was off sick. Bob had broken his ankle over the weekend, falling on the icy steps outside his home. Leslie Rhodes had informed us all with great delight that she was pregnant. Mike was already bleating about heading home for the holidays. I felt lousy; I had a head cold and sore throat.

So, I was sitting behind my desk, shoes off, feet up, nursing a cup of scalding hot cider. I stared at the gifts stacked under the ten-foot Christmas tree that Jacque had insisted on putting up in my office. *Bah humbug!*

No, I didn't mean it; it was just a thought that bounced in and out of my head. I actually love Christmas. Most years, I shut down the office a couple of days before the holiday and we take the eight or ten days off through New Year. I usually head out to the mountains of Colorado. They do it right up there: snow, skiing, grand lodges, huge fireplaces with logs burning, and all the food and drink.... Well, you get the idea.

This year, though, my heart wasn't in it. I needed rest more than I needed a vacation, especially one that would leave me more tired than I was before I left.

Hmmm, I have a nice home. I'll get some sleep, cook some good food, listen to some good music, and play a couple of rounds of golf with the old man. He'll like that, and so will I; it's been a while. I'll keep a log fire burning and enjoy a little good company....

The cell phone next to my feet on the desk rang, jerking me out of my reverie and startling the hell out of me. I almost fell out of my chair when my feet dropped to the floor as I reached forward to grab it. I really didn't want to talk to anyone... but it was Lieutenant Kate Gazzara, Chattanooga PD.

"Hey, Kate. What's up?"

"I need for you to do me a favor." She didn't wait for me to answer. "I'm at a crime scene, and I need you to take a look. It's not far. Can you come, right now?"

"Crime scene? What sort of crime scene?"

"You'll see when you get here. Can you come? I mean right now?"

I heaved a huge sigh. I was really warm and comfortable where I was, and it was sleeting outside, for God's sake.

"Where are you, Kate?"

"I'm on McCallie. Hill House. You know the old three-story house on top of the rise, the one they decided to demolish?"

"Huh, yes."

2

"I'm there. You'll see the tapes. I'm round back, and hurry the hell up. I need you here while the techs are still on site."

"Gimme five minutes. That's if the traffic allows." I disconnected without waiting for her to answer, grabbed my heavy L.L. Bean Storm Chaser boots, slipped them on, climbed into my Fjallraven coat, and adjusted the Blackhawk holster on my hip. I put on a pair of black leather gloves, looked longingly at the big leather chair, and sighed.

My name is Harry Starke. I run a private investigation agency in Chattanooga. I have a small suite of offices with a staff of nine just a couple of blocks from the Flatiron Building on Georgia, close to the action: the courts and law offices.

"Back soon," I said to Jacque as I headed out into the parking lot. "Cover for me, okay?" I didn't wait for an answer from her either.

The drive took a little more than five minutes. I swung right off McCallie and parked on the side street. It was kinda crowded: three cruisers, a crime scene rig, a couple of unmarked police units, and now me. I slammed the car door and walked up the driveway to the rear of the house. An old, dilapidated red and white Ford 150 pickup truck with a small trailer attached was parked close to the rear entrance.

A Honda generator in the truck bed was running quietly.

The house and its environs were a mess: overgrown, strewn with old concrete blocks, bricks, and chunks of concrete balustrade. Trash of every shape, size and composition littered the entire backyard and driveway. The house itself, a once proud antebellum mansion, was a ruin, a pre-Civil War structure that had seen many a renovation and just as many owners. But all that was long ago. The house had been vacant for almost ten years. Much of the concrete stucco had fallen off the walls, leaving the bricks exposed and the exterior facade looking like a vast jigsaw puzzle. The steps to the rear entrance were long gone. The semi-circular rear porch and the balcony above it were in a dangerous state of disrepair. The concrete balustrades had collapsed, and the entire porch structure appeared about ready to fall in on itself. So sad. With the steps gone, the only access to the house at the rear was down through the basement.

Kate was standing at the top of the basement steps, gnashing her teeth with impatience, and she wasn't alone. Detective Sergeant Lonnie Guest was at her side, that stupid, shit-eating grin plastered all over his face.

"Hey, Kate," I said. "That egg on your shirt, Lonnie?" He looked down. "Gotcha, Lonnie."

"You're an ass, Starke. One of these days...."

"Yeah, yeah, yeah," I said, slapping him affectionately on the shoulder. "When you're man enough, you'll be too old. Now, Kate. What the hell is this all about?"

"For Christ's sake, you two." Kate really was exasperated. "Don't get started. I'm in no mood for that kinda crap today. If you can't be civil, Sergeant, you can go wait in the car, and you, Starke," she said, grimly. "You can show him a little respect, too."

Hmmm. Not so easy, that. Respect has to be earned, and that fat son of a bitch hates my guts. I don't like him a whole hell of a lot myself either. Starke? What's that about? She never calls me that.

"Now, Kate," I said. "When did I ever not show the good sergeant the respect he deserves?" *A kind of sideways question, but what the hell.*

As always, even dressed for the weather as she was, she looked terrific. Almost six feet tall, slender, long tawny hair tied back in a ponytail, an oval face with high cheekbones, huge hazel eyes and a high forehead. She was wearing jeans tucked into a pair of Timberland boots, a white turtleneck sweater under a heavy, black North Face Denali coat, and a black wool hat.

"Save it, and come *on.*" She started down the concrete steps into the basement. I looked at Lonnie.

He stared back at me, shrugged, and started down after her. I followed as he picked his way carefully down the ten broken steps. The wooden door at the bottom was shattered, hanging off its hinges at a drunken angle. Someone had strung lights from the generator on the truck. It wasn't much, but there was enough light for us to pick our way through the filth and trash that littered the basement floor.

Kate led the way up a second set of concrete steps to what, back in the day, must have been the kitchen. Now it was a shell. Whatever wallpaper there might have been was long gone. The plaster was falling off the walls and ceiling, and there were holes in the floorboards. The cabinets and appliances were also long gone; even the doors were missing.

"Be careful," Kate said, as she started up the stairs to the second floor. "Only one of us on the stairs at a time. They could collapse under the weight of more than one person, so tread carefully."

One by one, we negotiated the rickety, wooden stairs until finally we stood together at one end of a long passageway that led from one side of the house to other. There was another floor above, but for now, we were where Kate wanted us to be.

The walls on either side were punctuated by doorways that led into what once must have been bedrooms, maybe even a bathroom or two. The rooms themselves were uninhabitable, except perhaps by itinerant crackheads and the inevitable rats. Here and there among the ruins lay filthy, befouled old mattresses, discarded clothing, used condoms, needles, and filthy rags that once might have been blankets. The air was rank with the stink of decay, rot and putrefaction. Obviously, until recently, the place had been a vast squat.

Lonnie and I followed Kate along the landing to a doorway that led into a huge room that took up the entire width of the house. It was at least forty by twenty-five, with twelve-foot high ceilings. The master bedroom, maybe? It was cold, icy cold. Most of the glass in the big windows was gone; the sleet blew in unrestricted and lay in inch-deep white semi-circles beneath the window openings.

Five techs and the medical examiner, Dr. Sheddon, were gathered around a section of the floor in front of a huge bay window. Lights on stands, powered by the generator outside, surrounded a section of the floor where the boards had been taken up. The boards now lay in a pile in the middle of the room.

Two more rough-looking individuals were seated on old five-gallon drums at the side of the room farthest from where the techs were at work. Owners of the truck, no doubt.

"Grab some covers," Kate said, reaching into a large open case.

I took off my coat and hung it on a nail on the doorframe, shivering. *Damn. It's too goddamn cold for this crap.*

It took no more than a couple of minutes before all three of us were dressed head to toe in Tyvek coveralls, booties, and gloves. For the most part, we covered up in silence, aware of the sullen stares from the two creatures sitting on the oil drums.

"Okay," I said. "What do we have?"

We joined the group at the hole in the floor. All of them, including Doc Sheddon, were on their knees, three on either side of the hole. The exposed, rough-sawn joists were heavy, at least four by twelves on twenty-inch centers. *Sheesh. They built 'em to last back in the day.* Something was wedged in the gap between two of the joists. It was wrapped in clear polythene sheeting, though age had not treated it well. It had degraded to a point where it was all but impossible to see through the several layers that surrounded the... thing.

"Hello, Kate, Lonnie," Sheddon said. "Hey, Harry. How's it hangin'?" I had to smile. Doc had been greeting me the same way for years and, as far as I knew, I was the only one he greeted that way.

"I'm good, Doc. What do you have?"

8

"See for yourself," he said, inching his way sideways on his knees to give me room to join him. The others made room for Kate and Lonnie, although he remained standing.

The polythene had been torn... no, it had been slit, and then pulled apart to reveal the skeletal remains of.... *Christ! I wonder if we'll ever know.*

"She was young, Harry," Sheddon said, staring thoughtfully down at the skull. "Sixteen to eighteen, I should say, from what I can see here, but young, for sure."

"She?" I asked. "You sure?"

"Yep. The ridges — temporal, orbital, super ciliary — are almost non-existent. They never are well defined, even in males, but in this case...."

"Any idea how long she's been here, Doc?" Kate asked.

"Hah. That's a difficult one, and one I'm not prepared to answer here, at least not with any precision. Could be as little as two years, or as many twenty. I'd gravitate to midway between the two: ten, maybe twelve years. She's naked, so clothing will be no help. I don't know. We may have to send her off to Knoxville for a definitive answer. Even then I'd say they wouldn't be able to date the PMI – the post mortem interval - conclusively, maybe within one or two years."

He looked up at Kate. "Catherine, my dear. I think you'll have to figure this one out using good old detective work, but that's what you two are good at, right? Well, good luck with that, my friends. I'll see what I can do to help, but we'll need to identify her first. I hope there's enough left of her to do so. I'll have her taken to my lab; we'll begin there. I don't have much on right now, so we can start as soon as you like. After lunch be okay? Say one o'clock?"

"Harry?" Kate asked.

"I... guess," I said, shaking my head.

Christ. The last thing I need is an afternoon in a freezing lab with a bag of old bones and... Lonnie.

"No pay, I suppose?" I said it to Kate, with a smile.

"Just the pleasure of my company," she replied.

We rose to our feet, walked a few steps, stopped, turned, and together we watched as Doc Sheddon stripped off his covers, bagged and sealed them, then gathered up his gear. He shambled off, muttering to himself, his long black overcoat and heavy case barely clearing the floor.

"I'll have the techs pull the rest of the boards. See if there's anything else hidden away." Kate looked thoughtfully around the big room and shrugged. "I suppose we need to have the entire building processed. Could be more bodies. Damn. That will take days, if not weeks. The chief will have a conniption. Shit."

She went and gave the instructions to the team, then came back shaking her head. "They are not happy. What with the weather and all, and I don't blame them, but it has to be done."

We stripped off our covers and left the techs working the scene. I grabbed my coat, put it on, fastened it all the way up to the neck, and then put on my gloves.

"So," I said to Kate. "I'm assuming those two lovely-looking characters over there found her, right?"

"Yeah. Apparently they'd heard that the house is to be demolished and figured they would steal the floorboards — heart pine, more than 150 years old, worth a fortune — but they got a nasty shock."

"So let's talk to them."

She nodded. "Okay, but they're not going to know anything."

We walked the few yards to where they were sitting, shivering. They had their elbows on their knees, hands clasped together, blowing on them. They looked up at us, scowled, but said nothing.

"So," Kate said. "What were you two heroes doing here?"

"We done tol' the officer," the bigger of the two said, waving a hand in the general direction of a uniformed policeman who had recently appeared in the doorway. "We tol' 'im we was gettin' a foo boards fur a frien' who makes furniture. Nice wood these; old-growth pine. Worth a dollar or two. Hell, they's gonna pull 'er down anyway. We'd gotten a foo of 'em up," he waved toward the pile of floorboards in the center of the room, "'an we figured just a foo more 'an we'd be outa 'ere. An' we finds it. Dint know whut it wus, till we cuts the plastic, like. Sheeit. Ah 'bout 'ad a 'art attack."

Good lord. Now those are two good old boys, that's for sure.

"Did you move anything; take anything off the body?" I asked.

"No sir," he said, shaking his head, vigorously. "Ah jus' cut the plastic, 'an then Ah jumped outa there and called 911. They tol' us to stay put, an' we did. Dint we, Chester?"

Chester nodded enthusiastically, chewing vigorously on something nasty. He turned his head, spit a stream of dark brown fluid onto the boards beside him, and looked up again, still chewing rapidly.

"Then you won't mind if we search you, right?" Kate asked.

12

They both looked warily at her, then slowly shook their heads.

"Stand up. Both of you," Kate said. "Lonnie." She twitched her head in Chester's direction.

Lonnie stepped forward. "*Do it!*" he growled, and they did.

He's an intimidating presence, is Lonnie Guest; a big man, not big tall, big fat. He's maybe five feet eleven and could probably do with losing fifty, maybe even sixty pounds. He's obnoxious, arrogant, and an enigma. He's not quite as stupid as he would have you believe; he's often given to rare and always unexpected bursts of brilliance. He doesn't like me worth a damn, but he tolerates me. Mostly because he knows Kate wouldn't have it any other way. He's useful, sometimes, when he's not wearing his perpetual shit-eating grin.

So, the two would-be floorboard thieves stood quietly while Lonnie slowly and thoroughly searched them. By the time he'd finished, they were standing before us wearing nothing but socks and filthy underwear, shivering.

"Nothing," Lonnie said, stepping away from them.

"Get dressed and get out of here," Kate said. "And be quick about it."

"Whut about our wood?" the big man said, through chattering teeth.

"I'm going to pretend I didn't hear that," she said. "The wood is not yours. It belongs to the property owner, and I'm sure he, or she, has plans for it. If you'd been caught stealing it, you were looking at a couple of years in Silverdale. As it is, you can go, and be thankful. Oh, and we'll need to borrow the generator. You can pick it up at the lot tomorrow morning."

"But, but, but...."

"No buts, dickhead," Lonnie said. "Just go take the genny out of the truck and leave before the lieutenant changes her mind. Gimme your full name, address and phone number, and I'll see the supervisor at the lot has it when you go pick it up."

They shambled off, along the landing toward the stairs, muttering to each other.

"That was a little harsh, don't you think?" I said to Kate. "After all, they did call it in. God only knows when and what we would have found if they hadn't."

She didn't answer. She just shrugged and walked back across the room to the hole in the floor where the techs were easing the fragile package out from between the joists.

They laid it gently on the floor and stepped away. We all stood in a circle around it, looking down upon the pathetic little bundle that once had been a young woman, full of life, and maybe dreams of something special. It never failed to affect me.

How do they do it? I've seen it so many times. How does someone intentionally take the life of another human being? Assuming it was murder, that is.

I looked at Kate. Her face was pale, her lips clamped tight together, and her brow furrowed. She must have felt me staring at her, because she looked at me, turned the corners of her mouth down, and shook her head.

"C'mon," she whispered. "Let's get out of here. I need a drink."

Chapter 2

We didn't feel much like eating, but we were cold, so we headed to the Billiard Club on Jordan Avenue. The drive took less than ten minutes, and it was still early when we arrived. The place was almost deserted. Kate parked the unmarked in the lot, and I parked beside her.

"When are you going to get yourself a decent car, Starke?" Lonnie asked as we walked across the lot. "Hell, you should be driving a Porsche instead of that piece o' shit Maxima."

Kate smiled, and so did I.

"You're right, Lonnie. I could have a Porsche if I wanted one, but I don't. They attract too much attention. The piece of shit Maxima would surprise you — zero to sixty in five point three seconds — and it's low profile; nobody notices it. Ever tried surveillance in a sports car, Lonnie? Once is enough, let me tell you. Besides, I never did put much stock in expensive automobiles. Quickest way I know to throw money away."

He snorted. "I had your kinda money, I'd be drivin' a Ferrari."

I smiled, but didn't answer.

We ordered burgers and fries all round, a Bud each for the two cops, and a Blue Moon for me, no orange slice. As the lunchtime crowd had yet to arrive, we were able to find a small, round table in what we hoped would be a quiet corner.

I felt a little uncomfortable, sitting at the same table as Lonnie, especially with Kate, but there was no other choice.

We go back a long way, Kate and I, more than fifteen years, in fact, since she was a rookie cop. We'd been more than just associates, too, until I screwed things up. We were still friends, and we still worked together, now and then. I was a cop before I was a PI, and she sometimes called me in as a consultant, unpaid of course. This was one of those times, although I have a feeling that Kate's boss, Chief Johnston, would have put a stop to it if the collaboration wasn't so productive.

"So, Harry, what do you think?" Kate asked, over the neck of her beer bottle.

"About the body? I have no idea. We need to wait and see what Doc Sheddon finds. How long has Hill House been vacant?"

"A long time," Lonnie said. "Seven or eight years, at least. A skanky woman crackhead broke an arm when she fell down those basement stairs a few weeks ago, so the council decided it was a danger to the public and an eyesore, and that it should be demolished."

"Yeah," I said. "I knew that. I saw it in the *Times* a couple of weeks ago. Shame. It must have been quite something in its day. If that body has been under the floor for ten or more years, she must have been put there when the house was occupied. We need to find out about its owners, who they were and where they are now. We also need to know exactly what the house was being used for over the last twenty years or so, and when it became vacant. I heard it was some kind of shelter, or rehab."

"Some organization for battered and abused women, I think it was last," Lonnie mumbled, through a mouthful of burger. "Before that it was a homeless shelter. Before that... I dunno." *Christ. Didn't anybody ever teach him any manners?*

"Well," Kate said. "That's a start, but we'll need specifics, firm dates, names, and so on. Lonnie, when we get out of here, I want you to go to the records office and get everything you can. I want it all, so do a good job. Take my car."

"But...."

"Yeah, I know," she said. "You wanted to be present at the autopsy. Wow, you really are a morbid son of a bitch. I wish I could trade places with you, but I can't. So you're it. Just suck it up and do it."

He grunted something and took a huge bite of his burger. He chewed noisily, washed it down with a huge pull from his beer, and then stuffed a huge handful of fries into his mouth. He reminded me of a pig at the trough. *Nasty!*

He shoved his stool away from the table, rose to his feet, belched quietly, adjusted his belt, and smiled benignly at Kate. "Okay, then. I'll take the car and head on down to the courthouse, right?"

She nodded. "Yes. I'll ride with Harry to the Forensic Center. Don't take all day, Lonnie. I'll meet you back at the office, say... at four."

He nodded and shambled away. Somehow, in a confined space, Lonnie appeared larger than life and, dressed as he was in a quilted cold-weather jacket, he looked enormous.

"How the hell do you put up with him, Kate?"

"Oh, he's not so bad. He tries hard, most of the time. He can get on your nerves, though."

"He's a slob," I said.

She looked at her watch. "Time to go. We don't want to keep the old man waiting."

The old man was just finishing his lunch when we arrived. He was seated at his desk, eating from a box of McNuggets and sipping something through a straw from a blue plastic cup with a picture of a happy Fozzie Bear. Seated across from him was Carol Owens, the center's forensic anthropologist. She was nursing a cup of coffee.

19

Carol — Bones, as Doc Sheddon insists on calling her — is a sweet lady in her late forties, a bit of a geek, with an inordinate sense of humor. I suppose you'd need one if you spent your days sorting through the bones of the dead, as she does.

"Hey, you two," Sheddon said, flapping a hand in the direction of two chairs. "Come on in and sit you down. I'll be finished in minute. You want coffee? No? Okay."

"So," Carol said. "How is it with Samson and Delilah? Haven't seen you two in a while."

Samson and Delilah? That's a first.

Kate looked at me and smiled. Then she looked at Carol and shrugged. "Okay, I guess."

The small talk went on for several minutes more until Doc Sheddon finally popped the last of the nuggets into his mouth, pushed everything away from him, and stood up. His seat scraped the floor noisily as he shoved it away with the backs of his knees.

"Let's go take a look, then," he said.

The remains were on one of the stainless steel autopsy tables. Carol had opened the plastic sheeting and exposed the bones. They were a pathetic sight to be sure: blackened, some of the ribs were broken, scraps of mummified material still adhered to some of the ribs and long bones, matted hair around and beneath the skull.

All of a sudden, I felt very depressed. This poor soul was someone's daughter. How the hell does anyone cope with something like this?

"As you can see, there's not much left of her," Sheddon began. "The environment was nice and dry, at least most of the time, so the corpse is partly skeletonized and partially mummified. Many of the tendons and ligaments have decayed, thus some of the bones have separated. The jawbone is no longer attached to the skull, and some of the teeth have come loose. She's not much more than a pile of bones. That being so, there's not much I can tell you, other than that she was strangled to death, probably manually. The hyoid bone... there, you see?"

He pointed with his pen to a U-shaped scrap of bone, barely distinguishable among the debris.

"It's damaged, cracked in two places, by someone's thumbs, I shouldn't wonder. Other than that, there are no obvious signs of blunt or sharp force trauma."

He paused, shook his head, obviously saddened.

"I don't think she was much more than a teenager, probably sixteen or seventeen, maybe even eighteen, but no more than that. Five feet six inches tall. She hadn't finished growing. African-American.

Black hair. Weight? Hard to tell, but probably between 120 and 140 pounds. PMI? I dunno... at least not with any specificity. The plastic wasn't wrapped tightly, so air, insects, and atmospheric conditions played a part in the decomposition. I'd say nine to twelve years."

"What about identification?" Kate asked. "DNA, surely?"

"Yes. The teeth are intact, so we have enough material for a DNA analysis, so that might help. We've also taken care to preserve the integrity of the plastic. When we've finished with it, I'll have it sent for fingerprinting. Maybe you'll catch a break. There's not enough material left on the fingers to print, so that's not an option. Teeth? There are a couple of fillings that might come in handy — numbers thirteen and fifteen — and there's an old scaphoid fracture of the left wrist; a fairly common injury, especially among young and athletic folk. As I said, not much to work with, but it's something. Good luck to you both. Oh, one more thing...."

He picked up a small evidence envelope from the table and handed it to Kate. She opened it, peeked inside, and then looked questioningly at Sheddon.

"She was wearing the necklace, and the ring was on the middle finger of her right hand. It's a man's signet ring. Gold, I think, with what looks like the letters RJ engraved on it. The necklace is silver, tarnished, almost black. Might help, if you ever figure out who she is."

Kate handed the envelope to me. Inside were two small, plastic baggies. One held the ring, the other the necklace, a slim chain with a tiny cross.

"She's African-American?" I asked. "How can you tell? What I see there looks barely human."

"People of African descent often have slightly curled surfaces on the rear edges of their jaws... here, you see?" He pointed with his pen, looked up at me, and then shook his head. "No, of course you don't," he said, reasonably. "You'll just have to trust me. Caucasian jaws are more likely to have a flatter edge, and there are other slight differences, too."

"So," Kate said. "We have an average-sized, African-American teenage girl, strangled, dead at least ten years, maybe more, a couple of fillings, a broken wrist, fully healed, a man's gold ring, a silver cross and chain, and that's about it, right?"

"Yup. Sorry I can't be more specific. If you can come up with something... maybe I can do better. As it is...."

"How about a reconstruction?" I asked.

"Of the head, you mean?" Sheddon asked. "I don't see why not. The skull is in good condition; no damage. They have some talented folk at UT. Why don't you look into it? Carol can make a cast for you. Here she is. Why don't you ask her?"

"Hey, Carol," I said. "What are the chances of you making us a plaster cast of the skull? I'd like to see if we can get a reconstruction done."

"Quite good, I would think. As soon as Doc gives the all clear, I'll get right on it." Carol looked at him.

He shrugged, shook his head. "Not today. We should be through here early this evening. Then you can have at it."

"It shouldn't take more than a day or two," Carol said. "Whom do you have in mind for the reconstruction? If you don't have anyone, I know a very good artist, and she's quite reasonable."

"I'll bear that in mind, Carol," I said. "In the meantime, I need to check one or two other options. Let me get back to you on it. And the cast? You'll call me when it's ready?"

"Of course." She turned to the table and began gently to strip away the plastic sheeting. I could see by the way she was teasing it off the bones and mummified material that it would be a long job.

I handed the envelope back to Sheddon, who placed it back on the table. I looked again the remains. *Bastards. Who were you, sweetheart?*

I shuddered. It was as if someone had dropped a cube of ice down my back.

"I've seen enough," I said. "Let's get the hell out of here." I didn't wait for an answer. I was angry. No, I was pissed off, big time. I turned and walked out of the lab, out of the building, got into my car, turned up the radio, and waited for Kate.

"What the hell is wrong with you?" she asked, as she slammed the car door.

"Christ, Kate. What the hell do you think is wrong with me? Did that not have any effect on you whatsoever? That was someone's daughter. Some lousy, godforsaken bastard stole the poor kid's life, not to mention what he did to her first. And then he stuffed her under the floor, like a piece of garbage."

Her face was somber, set, her lips clamped together, pale and bloodless. "I've seen too many of them, and so have you. You get used to it; you know that. Lighten up."

I heard it, but I knew she didn't mean it. She was as pissed as I was, but she wasn't going to admit it; not to me.

Chapter 3

At four o'clock, we were seated together in Kate's office, Lonnie Guest included. He with his usual stupid grin on his face, Kate looking decidedly down in the dumps, and me... I was thoroughly depressed.

"So what did you find out, Lonnie?" Kate asked.

He rifled through several grubby pages of a small spiral-bound notebook. "The house was built in 1843. It was used as a Union Hospital during the siege of Chattanooga in 1863. Since then, it's changed owners many times. Right now, the property is owned by the Clermont Foundation. They purchased it in June of 2005 and used it as a shelter for abused women and children. It was a dump even then, too far gone and too expensive to properly renovate. They moved out in October of 2008. They still own it, but the house has been vacant ever since, except for bums, druggies, and the like. A demolition order was issued three weeks ago, and they are actively taking contractor bids."

"Who and what is the Clermont Foundation?" I asked.

"It's a charitable organization run by a doctor and his wife. They still run the shelter, but now it's located in a bigger, more modern building off East

Brainerd Road. Dr. Draycott, his name is. I have contact details for you."

"And before that?" Kate asked.

"From 1946 until the Draycotts purchased the house, it was owned by the Vickers family. Mrs. James Vickers moved out when her husband died in 1969, and it became a part of the Vickers' family trust, which was administered by Turnbull and Turnbull; a law firm. They employed a property manager, Wilson Jennings, who rented the house to a Mr. William Dickerson, who ran it as a kind of... I don't know what to call it. A sort of homeless shelter, maybe. No official standing. He just took folks in and financed the thing by charitable donations. He did that until the trust sold the house to the Draycotts in June 2005."

"Damn it," I said. "So we have a double window of opportunity."

"What do you mean?" Lonnie asked.

"He means," Kate said, "that if the girl died ten years ago, give or take two or three years; it could have happened on either watch; when it was a drug rehab or the shelter. She could have been killed prior to or after June 2005, when the property changed hands. That complicates things."

Lonnie stared down at his notes, shaking his head. "Yeah. I see what you mean."

"Well," I said, "solving a murder, any murder, is totally dependent on our being able to identify the victim. If we can't identify her, we'll have a hell of a job figuring out who killed her."

"So where do we start?" Lonnie asked.

"I'd say we need to start with the missing person data bases. Tim's specialty, right?" Kate asked, and looked at me.

"Yes. I'll head back to the office and get him started on it. What are you going to do?"

"Unfortunately, I have a pile of urgent stuff to work my way through, and so do you, Lonnie. Sorry, Harry. It's an old case, and we don't even have an ID on the victim. Same old same old, so I can't devote much time to this one. I've okayed it with Chief Johnston so, for the moment, you're it. That's why I called you this morning. You're a sucker for cold cases, and they don't come much colder than this. Do you want it?"

I nodded. "Yeah, well, someone needs to be held accountable, and I get the feeling that if it's not handled quickly, it will be set aside and forgotten, and that's not right." I paused, thinking about the pathetic little pile of blackened bones on Doc Sheddon's table. I shook my head, trying to rid myself of a whole host of terrible images, but they wouldn't go.

"Hell, yeah, I want it," I said. "Just let me know if CSI finds anything else, yeah? Oh, and if you would, email me a photo of the ring and the necklace. You never know, they might come in handy."

"Yeah, I'll do that, probably later today, before I send them for processing," she said. "In the meantime, let's stay in touch, okay?"

I nodded. "Give us a minute, would you, Lonnie?"

He ginned, heaved himself out of his seat, and left, closing the door behind him.

"So," I said. "What are your plans for tonight?"

"We're short-handed. I have to work until midnight. Why?"

"Oh... I dunno. Thought you might want to... get together, for dinner, maybe."

I felt kind of stupid asking, but what the hell. It was worth a shot. It had been more than a month since the last time. We had a strange relationship, Kate and I. Ever since that deal with Olivia Hansen back in January, things had not been the same between us. Oh, we saw plenty of each other, but only on her terms. *You ever get the feeling you're being used? Maybe it's time I gave it up; let her go.*

She heaved one of those big sighs, shook her head, looked down at the open pad on her desk, scribbled something, and then looked back up at me.

"Not tonight. I have to be here. Tomorrow, though, maybe. What did you have in mind? Oh no you don't," she said as I was about to make a smart remark. "Dinner, or a few drinks. That's all."

I shrugged. "That will work. I'll book a table at the club. Seven be okay?"

She nodded.

"Good. I'll pick you up. If anything breaks, you know how to reach me."

Five minutes later, I was in my car, heading south on Riverside Drive.

Chapter 4

I walked into my office that afternoon and remembered that my staff was down by two. My lead investigators were both off: Bob Ryan with a broken ankle and Heather Stillwell was 'sick.'

"Jacque," I said. "What's wrong with Heather? Can you find out?"

Jacque Hale is my personal assistant, been with me almost from the beginning, even before she got out of college. She's Jamaican, though she doesn't have much of an accent, twenty-seven years old, has a great sense of humor and a wonderful personality. However, she can be a real... well, you know, when things don't go just exactly as they should.

"I already know," she replied. "She has the flu. She came in early, but I sent her home, told her to stay away until she was better."

"Well good. I sure as hell don't need to catch it. What about Bob?"

"He'll be back tomorrow: walking wounded, complete with cane."

I grinned at that one. *Bob with a cane. The man's a bear. That I have to see.*

I grabbed a cup of dark roast at the Keurig, then turned and walked to where Tim was pounding away on his keyboard.

"Hey," I said, laying a gentle hand on his shoulder.

He almost jumped out of his seat.

"Sorry, Tim. Didn't mean to startle you. We need to talk. Grab a coffee and come on into my office. You'll need to make notes."

Tim Clarke is my geeky computer guy. He's been hacking since he was able to sit up straight; never got caught. Now he's reformed. *At least I think he is.* He handles all things to do with the Internet, including operating and maintaining the company website. He also handles background checks and skip searches. He can find people, addresses, phone numbers, you name it. I said he was geeky, and I meant it: he's tall, skinny, wears glasses, is twenty-five years old and talks a language known only to himself. He's also the busiest member of my staff.

I was just about to go looking for him when he came backing in through the door, his hair hanging down over his eyes, a pen between his teeth, and a notepad under his arm. A laptop balanced precariously in the crook of his left arm, and there was an overflowing cup of coffee in his right hand.

He set the laptop and cup on the edge of my desk, took the pen from his mouth, pulled up a chair, sat down, and grinned.

I gazed back at him in awe, shook my head, leaned back in my chair, and sipped on my own cup of coffee. "I need to think about getting you some help."

"Funny you should say that," he said. "I know just the right person. She's—"

"Oh you do, do you?" I interrupted. "I didn't say I would. I said I needed to think about it."

"Yeah, but she's—"

"Forget it, Tim. I'll talk to Jacque about it, later."

"But...." He saw the look in my eye and decided to let it go. "Okay, what do you need, Boss?"

"They've found the body of a young girl under the floor in Hill House."

"How old?" He dumped his cup down on my desk, coffee splashing up and over the rim, making a pool around it on the walnut top. Then he slid the laptop toward him. "Ethnicity? How tall? Weight? Distinguishing marks?"

"Christ, Tim. Calm down, slow down. Do you need a Zanex or something? If you'll give me time to talk, I'll give you the details. There are no distinguishing marks; she's partly mummified and more than half skeleton." I tried, with a handful of tissues, to keep the mess from running over the edge of the desk and down onto the carpet. *Geeze, the boy's hyper today.*

Oh," he said, his hands poised like two talons over the keyboard. "So what am I looking for, then?"

I sat back down, shook my head and glared at him. It didn't faze him a bit. He just grinned cheekily back at me.

I sighed. "She's African-American, aged between sixteen and twenty, five feet six tall. Been dead between eight and twelve years, but it's hard to tell, so you can add a couple of years on either end."

"Tattoos, scars, anything like that?" His fingers were already flying over the keys.

"No, there's not enough left of her. She does have a couple of fillings — numbers thirteen and fifteen — and there's an old scaphoid fracture of the left wrist, and… *Stop!*"

He stopped.

"I didn't mean for you to do it right now, and especially not here in my office. Just give me your first impressions and then get out of here and let me think, okay?"

"Sure… yeah… okay then. If she's local, it shouldn't be too difficult. Depends on if she was reported missing or not. If she wasn't…. Well, I'll do my best." He started to rise from the chair, then sat down again. "Is that all you have? No clothes? No jewelry? It's not much, and she's been dead a long time."

I nodded. "Do your best. There's a ring, a man's signet ring, and a necklace, but I'm waiting for photos of them. No clothes."

"What else?"

"I need to know about anyone who was associated with Hill House during the five years from 2003 through 2008. That would include the Draycotts, who still own the place, and the Dickersons, who were there until June of 2005. I want names of staff members, family members, with personal details, phone numbers, addresses, everything. Hell, I don't have to tell you what I want. Now get out of here and get on with it. Let me know as soon as you find anything."

He took his gear with him, left the half-empty cup with me, and closed the door behind him.

Now I was even more depressed. It hadn't hit me just how little we did have until I'd handed it off to Tim.

I sat staring up at the Christmas tree, cradling my cup in both hands, thinking about that dismal place where the poor girl had ended her days, laid like a sack of garbage all those years.

Son of a bitch! How can they do it? How can someone end a life and go on with their own as if... as if... shit, as if the poor kid had never existed. Someone did this. Someone killed her and stuffed her under the boards of that filthy place, among the rats and God only knows what else. Well, you piece of crap, I'm gonna find you, and when I do....

I was jerked out of it by a knock on the door.

"Yeah? Come on in."

The door opened a crack, and Jacque peeked in. "Amanda Cole is in the outer office. She wants to see you. Shall I send her in?"

"Yes, send her in. Ask her if she wants coffee."

Amanda Cole is one of lights in my life. The other two are Kate Gazzara and Senator Linda Michaels, whom I hadn't seen in more than a month.

One of the anchors at Channel 7 Television, Amanda is an inordinately beautiful woman. She wears her strawberry blonde hair bobbed, cut three inches below the point of her chin. Her heart-shaped face is defined by high cheekbones and wide-set, pale green eyes. She's thirty-two years old and, as far as I know, she's never been married.

A couple of years ago, she did an on-air hatchet job on me, calling me a predator and a bounty hunter with the conscience of a grizzly bear. From that point on, I had avoided her. I swore I'd never give her the chance to do it again. Five months ago, I hated the sight of her, much less did I want to spend time with her. Funny how things change. These days, I probably spend more time with her than I should, but her presence is infectious. No, damn it, the woman is addictive.

Back in August, she'd somehow talked me into letting her work with me on a case and, well, one thing led to another, and here we were.

She wore her signature, navy blue two-piece business suit with the skirt cut four inches above the knee, and black high heel shoes. Over the suit, she had on a double-breasted, blue and white hounds' tooth coat. Stunning.

She waited until the door had closed, then took off the coat and walked around the desk. She hitched up her skirt, straddled me, wrapped her arms around my neck, put her lips on mine and gifted me with a kiss that all but sucked the life out of me. She broke the hold, stepped away from me, walked back around the desk and dropped heavily into the seat that Tim had not long ago vacated.

"Damn," she said, looking up at me through half-closed eyes, "I needed that."

"Hello, Amanda. Having a good day, are we?"

"We are now," she said. "Where are you taking me tonight?"

"Taking you? I haven't seen or heard from you in nearly a week and you walk in here and.... Yeah, okay. Where do you want to go?"

"Hmmm... somewhere nice and quiet. Let me think.... Oh yes, I know. Your place or mine. It doesn't matter. I need to get laid in the worst way. Oh my God. Now that sounds terrible," she said, laughing. "Not the worst way, the best way. In fact, any way you want. You up for it?"

Now she really was laughing, one double *etendre* after another.

"Oh, I dunno," I said, off handedly. "Let me think about it.... Eeh... well, okay."

"You shithead," she laughed. "Come on. Let's get out of here. We can go to the club. Have a few drinks and a nice early dinner. What do you say?"

I thought about for a minute and nodded. "Okay, but I'm gonna pick your brains."

"Nooo, Harry. I don't want to talk shop. I just want to have a nice evening."

"And so do I, but this is important, and I think it will interest you, too. There may be... no, I know there will be a story in it for you. Then," I heaved a sigh as if I was giving in to some unpleasant task, "we can go play."

That brought a smile to her lovely face. "Okay, let's go."

Twenty minutes later, we were at the club seated together in the booth overlooking the ninth green. I'd just ordered drinks — a vodka tonic for Amanda and a Blue Moon beer, no slice of orange, for me — when we were interrupted.

"Hello, you two. Bit early, isn't it?"

"Hey, Dad." I stood up and shook hands with my father.

My father, August Starke, is a lawyer, a very good one. He specializes in tort, which is a classy word for personal injury. You've probably seen him on TV. His ads run on most local stations almost every day; that damn jingle embarrasses the hell out of me, but that's Dad; he's a showman, larger than life, and rich as Croesus. He's an inch taller than I am, with silver hair, not unlike like the Donald's. He's fit, toned, with not a pound of extra fat on him anywhere. He was dressed for golf: a black Nike golf shirt, accented by a gold chain around his neck, white Fila slacks, and a pair of white ECCO Evo shoes. He dresses well, does my old dad.

"Early? Maybe, but who cares? You know Amanda Cole, of course," I said.

"I do. How are you, Amanda?"

"Not so well as you, Colonel. Please, join us for a drink, won't you?" *Colonel? Nobody calls him that anymore.*

"Well... just one then, if that's all right with you, son."

Oh it's fine with me, but 'just one'? Come on. That will be a first.

"Of course," I said. "What will you have?"

He had a dry martini; the first of four, but I wasn't complaining. My father is great company, and I wanted to pick his brains, too.

We made small talk for a few minutes, mostly about the old man's golf game — he's very proud of his five handicap — and then I dragged them both back to reality.

"What do you know about Hill House?" I threw it out there, hoping one of them would know something. One did.

"Hill House?" Amanda asked. "You mean that derelict monstrosity on McCallie?"

"Yeah, that one," I said.

My father leaned back in his seat, spinning the stem of his empty martini glass between his fingers, a strange, faraway look on his face.

"It's scheduled for demolition," Amanda said, "so I heard. Why do you ask?"

"They discovered the body of a young girl there yesterday morning. Kate has the case, among a host of others, and she asked me to see what I could find out. If you hadn't come by the office, I would have called you anyway."

"Well... I'm not sure what I know. It's been vacant for a long time and is in a terrible state. Wasn't it a shelter of some sort, a few years ago?"

"Yes, it was," I said. "From 2005 until 2008. It's been vacant ever since. Prior to 2005, it was a rehab of some sort."

"That's right. I remember." She sat up straight, put her glass down on the table, and then shoved it my direction.

I took the hint and waved at Joe. He nodded and began to prepare another round of drinks.

"The rehab was run by a very dubious character... Nicholson... I think his name was, or something similar." She screwed up her face as she concentrated. If anything, it made her look even more beautiful.

"Dickerson," I said. "William Dickerson. Tim's running a check on him. What the hell do you have on your mind, Dad?" He was staring, unblinking, out of the window.

"Oh, I was just thinking of times past. I spent several weekends in that house, back in the day when it was something special. My best friend at the time was James Vickers; his family owned the place. We were at McCallie together. Happy times those.

Unfortunately, James was killed during the latter days of the Viet Nam war. Poor Lucy never got over it. She died last year. She was only sixty-two, bless her. Oh well. I'm sorry. Please continue, Amanda."

"Dickerson you say his name was, Harry?" She looked at me quizzically, her eyebrows raised.

I nodded.

"Well, from what I remember, there was some sort of scandal and the place had to be closed. Sexual abuse of patients, as I recall. I'd have to do a little digging through our archives, but I'm sure I could find it. What do you know about the girl, Harry?"

Not much. I filled them in on the details. By the time I'd finished, we were all depressed. I signaled Joe and ordered another round of drinks.

The drinks came and were consumed, for the most part, in silence. I looked at my watch. It was almost seven.

"You want to join us for dinner?" I asked him.

He sighed. "No, I don't think so. I'm sure you two have better things to do than sit around gassing with an old duffer like me." He tipped up his glass, drained it, set it back on the table, and rose to his feet.

"Call me tomorrow, Harry. Goodnight, Amanda. It was nice to see you again." He turned away from the table without waiting for an answer and walked out into the lobby, leaving us staring after him.

We ordered dinner, but our appetites were not what they had been a couple of hours earlier, at least mine wasn't. I didn't enjoy my steak and I left most of it. Amanda? Well, appetite or not, she managed to down a ten-ounce fillet with red potatoes and asparagus.

We left the club a little before ten o'clock. I drove Amanda's Lexus back to my place. I'd left my car back at the office on Georgia, and neither of us was in a fit state to go get it. Be that as it may, we arrived at my home on Lakeshore Lane safely, and to both of our reliefs. I sure as hell didn't need a DUI on my record, and neither did Amanda.

I opened a bottle of Niersteiner, and we settled down of the sofa in front of the big windows, Amanda's head on my shoulder. A strong breeze blowing across the surface of the water had turned the river into a living thing, a vast expanse of rippling whitecaps that glittered and glistened in the moonlight.

I looked down at Amanda; she was fast asleep, her glass still clamped tight in her fingers. I took it gently from her, set it on the coffee table, and lowered her gently onto the cushions. I fetched a blanket, covered her, and then I went to the bedroom, stripped and crawled under the covers. It was four-thirty in the morning when I awoke as she crawled into bed beside me, naked. In less than thirty seconds, she was asleep again.

The next thing I knew was the buzz of my cell phone on the nightstand. It was eight-thirty, and Jacque wanted to know where the hell I was. I told her I'd be in later, turned off the phone, and then I fulfilled my promise to Amanda.

Chapter 5

I finally arrived at my office around eleven that morning: not good, and Jacque let me know it. I hadn't been seated at my desk for more than a couple of minutes when my office door opened and she stormed in, her face like thunder. She said not a word as she dumped a pile of papers on my desk. I looked up at her and grinned; she didn't smile back. She simply spun on her heel and flounced back out into the outer office, closing the door behind her. She didn't exactly slam it, but she could have done it more quietly. *Sheesh, the stuff I have to put up with.*

I looked down at the heap of papers. Most of it I knew I could sign off on and send back to Jacque to deal with. There, however, several phone messages. All of which needed my immediate attention. The most pressing of which were no less than three calls from Kate. *What the hell's up with her?*

I turned on my phone and dialed her cell number; she answered immediately.

"Damnit, Harry. Where the hell have you been? I've called three times."

"Yeah, so I heard. I had stuff to take care of. Sorry. What's so urgent?"

"You need to get over here. CSI found some personal belongings. They were under the next section of the floor, right next to the body, in fact."

"Okay. I have a few things to take care of. Shouldn't take more than thirty minutes, and then I'll head on over there."

"Good, and turn your damn phone on."

"It's on. I'm talking to you on it...." *Damn, she hung up on me. What the hell's gotten into her, I wonder?*

I never did find out. By the time I arrived at the PD an hour later, she was her usual sunny but caustic self. I followed her to the crime lab where a tech had laid out the few pathetic belongings of what once had been a vibrant teenage girl.

None of it had weathered the years well. The cut-off jeans (Walmart brand), were filthy, covered in dust. A white T-shirt with the letters UTC on the front was in much the same condition, only now it was a dirty shade of gray. A white bra, also filthy, panties torn almost in half, and a pair of grubby, but obviously expensive, black leather sandals completed the count. To one side, the tech had also laid out the contents of the pockets: a bunch of four keys, a slim leather wallet (empty), some loose change, and that was it.

"UTC," I said. "That's something."

46

"Maybe, maybe not," Kate said. "Could have been a gift, or borrowed. Still.... Strange mix of clothing; the Walmart jeans and the shoes. They must have cost at least $100. As you said, though, it's not much."

"We have to find out who she was. Can't do much until we do. I'll get Tim to do some more digging. In the meantime, we need to run the missing person databases for the period 2003 through 2008. Maybe the two fillings and the broken wrist will throw something up."

With Kate watching, the tech bagged the pathetic few personal belongings of our Jane Doe, labeled the bags, and signed off on them; they had been entered into evidence.

"Let's get out of here," she said. "I've had enough of the cold, the smell, and the sight of... whoever she was."

I looked at my watch. It was almost one o'clock.

"Kate, I need to go back to the office; see what Tim has for me. You coming?"

"No. I have a huge backlog, and I need to do some catching up. If you need me, call, and for God's sake keep your damned phone turned on."

I opened my mouth to speak, but she continued, "Look. I don't mean to be a pain in the ass, and I really don't give a shit what you do with your time

47

off, or who you do it with, but if I need you, well, I need you. So please, keep it on. See yourself out, okay?"

She didn't give me a chance to say anything. She spun on her three-inch heels and walked rapidly away along the corridor, leaving me standing there, staring after her. *Geeze, she really* is *pissed off. Not good.*

Chapter 6

I drove slowly back to the office, stopping along the way to grab a Max Roast Beef sandwich at Arby's — I love those curly fries — and a tall iced tea. I didn't go in. I hit the drive through, and then parked the Maxima off to one side of the Arby's lot, turned on the radio, and settled down for a quiet moment. It lasted no more than that, a moment, before the Bluetooth cut the radio off.

"Hey, Mr. Starke. It's Tim. You got a minute?"

I sighed. "Yes, Tim. I always have time for you. What do you need?"

"I have some stuff for you. You know, what you were asking about. The Hill House people, an' that."

"Give me twenty minutes. I should be back in the office by then."

"You got it, Boss." He disconnected and the radio came on again, but I was in no mood to listen to it. I turned it off, hit the starter, drove out of the lot, and headed back to the office; my Max Roast Beef and Curly Fries would have to wait.

You know, there are times when I get really frustrated. There never seems to be a free moment. There's always someone wanting my time and attention; first Jacque, then Kate, and now Tim. *Damn, Harry. You need some time off, son.*

I thought about that. The problem is, I'm not a loner. I like having people around me. *Shit, Harry. That's a contradiction. No. That's different. Being at everyone's beck and call is one thing, good company when you want it, need it, is quite another.*

I was still daydreaming when I pulled into the office lot. The damn gates were wide open. *I need to fix that.*

"Jacque," I said, louder than I probably should have, "the damn gates were left open again. Put a stop to it, okay?"

Okay, maybe I was a little terse, but what the hell. *Do I have to do everything myself?*

I swept through the outer office, pointed at Tim as I went, then at the Keurig, then at my office door, which I flung open and then shut again. I threw my coat onto one of the easy chairs, then myself into my desk chair, and began to pick at the sandwich. The ill mood that had overcome me as I looked at the pathetic little pile of body parts earlier had turned into full-blown despondency. Not good.

The door opened and Tim came in, grinning like a fool. I opened my mouth to speak, thought better of it, and closed it again. He set the coffee down in front of me and then himself in the chair in front of my desk, his laptop on his knee, and looked at me expectantly.

"What?" I asked, with an edge to my voice. "You called me, remember?"

He blanched, looked quickly down at the keyboard, and then up again.

"I did, and I'm sorry. I didn't mean...." *Oh shit. Damn it, Harry.*

"No, Tim," I interrupted. "Don't go there. It isn't your fault. It's mine. I've had a rough day. I apologize. Now, what have you got for me?"

He took a deep breath, hit a couple of keys, and began. "Let's start with—"

"Wait. I think it would be a good idea if we got Bob and Heather in here. No point going over everything several times."

I punched the intercom button on the system phone and had Jacque ask them to join us. Bob, who limped in with the aid of his stick, was his usual brusque self; Heather was... still looking as if she needed to be home in bed.

"Heather. Should you even be here?" I asked. "You look like death warmed over."

"Gee, thanks, Boss. I needed those few words of encouragement and light. Yes. I feel okay. Head's a bit stuffed up, but other than that."

I looked doubtfully at her. Normally she's the poster girl for good health. I say girl; she's thirty-nine, but looks thirty; five feet eight tall, short brown

51

hair, an oval face, brown eyes, and a hard body she keeps well covered. She works out for an hour every morning, teaches self-defense in her spare time, and is an expert shot. She's also something of a mystery.

Heather Stillwell has worked for me for almost six years. Before she joined us, she'd spent the first two years of her law enforcement career as a street cop in Atlanta. From there, she was recruited into the GBI (Georgia Bureau of Investigation) and fast tracked for high office, but something happened. She never would talk about it. I'd met her on several occasions during the course of one investigation or another, and we hit it off immediately. *No, not like that. The lady is a pro, all cop, and you'd better believe it.*

One day, I got a call from her. She wanted to know if I had any openings. It happened right about the time things were beginning to move for my company. Bob and I were so busy we hadn't had a day off in months, so I hired her on the spot. To this day, I have no real idea why she left the GBI. I do suspect it was because of a personal relationship. Heather is gay, proud of it and, as far as I know, is not in a relationship now. She and Bob handle all of the field investigations.

Bob Ryan is my lead investigator. He's a year older than I am and has been with me almost since the day I first opened the agency. He, too, is an ex-cop – Chicago PD. He's also an ex-marine, stands six feet two and weighs in at more than 240 pounds – all of it solid muscle. He's quiet, dedicated, and not someone you want to screw around with.

I picked up the phone and and asked Mike to bring me a coffee. He did, and I told him to take a seat in the corner and listen. Bob, I knew, was already up to speed with the Hill House investigation, and I knew he would have taken the time to bring Heather into the loop as well.

"Okay, Tim," I said, when everyone had gotten settled. "Let's hear it."

"There are two previous owners of interest," he began. "I'll do this chronologically. From March 1998 until the end of May 2005, Hill House was occupied by a William Dickerson. Dickerson is a bit of an enigma. He has an arrest record going all the way back to the early 1980s, including six times for procuring and pimping, but he never served any time, for anything. All charges were pled down to misdemeanors. For five of them, he got off with a fine. For the last one in 2008, he was ordered to do 200 hours of community service. Does everyone know the difference between pimping and procuring?"

All of us ex cops did, but Mike held up his hand and said, "I don't."

Tim looked at me. I nodded. "The quick version, Tim."

"Pimping is receiving, either directly or indirectly, a prostitute's earnings, and that includes the act of asking for or receiving money in exchange for soliciting for a prostitute. Procuring is the practice of *procuring* a person to be used for, or to travel for, prostitution. It also includes running a brothel, and inducing, encouraging, or forcing someone to engage in or to continue to engage in prostitution. You don't have to pimp to be guilty of procuring, but the two almost always go hand-in-hand, For example, if someone tries to get a woman to work for him as a prostitute that's procuring, and if he then shares in her earnings, that's pimping. Got it?"

Mike nodded.

"Alrighty then. In Tennessee, both procuring and pimping are Class E felonies with penalties of one to six years in prison and, or, a fine of up to $3,000. Okay, back to Mr. Dickerson. There's little doubt that this man is at best shady, and at worst, well... something infinitely worse. Over the years, he's been connected to a whole nest of nefarious characters, including," he looked at me, "Salvatore De Luca."

"Sal De Luca?" *Son of a bitch. I thought I was done with that piece of shit.*

"Yep, him. Here," Tim said, "I have a photo of Dickerson as he was at his last arrest some seven years ago."

He handed large prints to each of us, including Mike. It was a mug shot and, as we all know, they are not the most flattering of portraits. This one ran true to form.

The head and shoulders image showed him to be five feet eight inches tall. He was white, unshaven, his hair was a wild nest of salt and pepper strands, some of which hung down around his ears, some over eyes that were narrowed almost to slits. The corners of his mouth were turned down in a scowl that was both ugly and scary.

"Nasty-looking son of a bitch," Heather said, frowning. "Who's he running with now, and what's he been up to lately?"

"Ah well, you see. That's what I meant about him being an enigma. He's still around, but no longer seems to generate interest among any of the law enforcement agencies. He's been clean for almost seven years, since his last arrest. Maybe you could get Kate to run him through their records, Harry."

I nodded and made the call on my cell phone. She picked up immediately. I explained what I needed, and she said she would get back to me as soon as she had something.

"But what's he doing?" Heather asked. "He has to be doing something to make a living. What is it?"

"Well, it seems to be more of the same. He used Hill House as a shelter of sorts, mostly for the homeless, especially girls, but he also took in addicts, mental cases, and so forth. It's hard to tell exactly what. Anyway, the Victor family lawyers kicked him out when they sold the property. These days, he has a place on Cherry Street. An old, two-story brick building that probably dates to the Civil War era."

"That's interesting," I said. "We have a dead girl hidden away in what was some sort of homeless shelter, or rehab. She one of the homeless, do you think?" It was a rhetorical question that required no answer; it got none.

"You can't run something like that without money," Bob said. "Who funded it?"

"Donations," Tim said. "He would send his inmates — maybe I should call them guests — out on the street panhandling. From what I've heard, he also had a small phone room operation that he used for fundraising. He was quite well organized; still is. These days, however, he calls himself Reverend Dickerson and his organization is called... wait for it.... 'Blessed are the Homeless'."

"Oh my God," Heather said. "Is it legit?"

"Seems to be. He houses up to twenty-five people at any one time. Has a staff of eight, including cooks and housekeepers."

"We need to talk to the Reverend Dickerson," I said. "Now, Tim, tell us about the Draycotts?"

"Now that's a strange one. It's a similar story, only they are much more upscale. Well, they weren't then, but they are now. They are also running a shelter. This one is called the Clermont Foundation and it's quite a sophisticated operation. It's a 501c3 nonprofit organization, as is the Reverend Dickerson's little operation. The Draycotts, though, provide, and I quote, 'emergency shelter, transitional housing, and supportive services to homeless girls'."

"Christ," Bob said. "Are you serious? Homeless girls?"

Tim nodded. "That I am. They have a large complex off East Brainerd Road: a single large block of living units and communal areas, and four separate quadraplexes on the grounds. It's a fairly substantial operation. They can handle up to sixty girls."

"And both the Draycotts and Dickerson started out in Hill House?" Heather asked.

"They did, and when Dickerson was thrown out, the Draycotts basically took over his operation, only with much more… how shall I say it? Okay, so theirs is a much more professional enterprise, and there's no drug rehab involved. They are, after all, both doctors: he's a family practitioner, she's a psychiatrist. They are well thought of in the community, and she belongs to several charitable institutions. Oh, and she's also sixteen years younger than he is; sixty-two to forty-six."

"So," I said, "they've been involved in caring for the homeless since 2005, when they bought Hill House?"

The intercom on my desk buzzed. I picked up.

"Amanda Cole is here to see you, Mr. Starke."

I looked at my watch; it was after three-thirty already. "Okay. Show her in, please, Jacque."

"Grab a seat, Amanda," I said when the door opened. "We were just talking about the history of Hill House, the Dickersons and the Draycotts in particular."

"Well, good afternoon to you, too, Harry," she said, with a grin. "Hello, Heather. Feeling better, I hope. Tim, Bob. Don't mind me," she said, pulling up a chair. "Hey, Mike."

Mike grinned at her, blushed, and looked stupid. The boy had an enormous crush on her.

"Go on, Tim," I said.

"Well, the Draycotts bought the place for next to nothing, $88,000, in June 2005, but it was in poor shape and in need of major renovations. They did some work on the house, but it seems they were unable to satisfy the code inspectors, and they were outgrowing it. They tried to sell it, but couldn't. In the end, they simply walked out, abandoned it. They still own it and will have to reimburse the city for the demolition."

I looked across the desk at Amanda. "Were you able to find anything?"

She shrugged, took out an iPad and turned it on. "Not much. There were all sorts of problems during Dickerson's tenure. The police were called on several occasions, and Dickerson and some of his cronies were arrested and hauled off. There were rumors of sexual and physical abuse, prostitution, complaints by neighbors, and even the residents. It all generated a lot of gossip and ongoing media attention, which led to the Vickers' family wanting to get rid of the place. And get rid of it they did, in 2005. How the hell they managed to find the Draycotts is unknown, but it can't be a coincidence that they were in the same line of business. From what I've been able to learn, it was an almost seamless turnover from Dickerson to Draycott; they even managed to hang on to some of the residents. Dickerson got away with murder.... Uh oh, wrong choice of words. We don't know that yet, do we?" She smiled as she said it, but it was obvious where she was going with it.

"And then we come right to the present. Our friend, the erstwhile *Reverend* William Dickerson is back at it. You know he has a place on Cherry, right?"

I nodded.

"At the last count," she continued, "he was housing fourteen young girls and women aged fifteen to twenty-one, plus five young girls aged between eleven and fourteen, and six young men, all of them, and I quote, *homeless*. It seems the reverend has built himself quite a dedicated little following."

She paused, took a sip of coffee, looked at me, and winked.

""Are there no concerns by the authorities that a known procurer is running a facility for homeless girls?" Heather asked.

"Apparently not," I said, "and that's a problem in itself. Sorry, Amanda. Go on."

"Oh you'll love this," she said. "He has a staff of eight, if you can call them that. His wife, India, manages the running of the place and the finances. He employs three 'handymen,' and I use that word loosely, Darius 'Romeo' Willett, Woody Handles, and Mickey Donavan, known among his peers as The Mouse, and a driver, Jack Harris."

"Hah," I said. "I know him. He's a little weasel. They call him Little Jacky. I've seen him at the

Sorbonne. Always accompanied by a woman, skanky-looking, older than him; a lot older. Strange pair."

"There's also a cook," Amanda continued, "Wanda Grindel, two housekeepers and two maids, all four are sort of girl Fridays, who handle general cleaning and serving meals. Back in the late 1880s, an establishment like this would have been called a workhouse. Today, it's a shelter and, I shouldn't wonder, the beginning of the end for many a disenfranchised young girl. Dickerson is a... procurer, pure and simple. He needs to be stopped."

She closed the cover on her iPad and looked across the desk at me. "That's all I have. There's much more, I'm sure, but it's beyond me. You, Harry, *I'm sure*, can get Kate to access his file at the PD."

I'm not sure I like the way she said that. What's she getting at, I wonder?

"One more thing," she said, almost as an afterthought. "He has some very wicked friends. Some of whom you all know, including Sal De Luca."

I nodded. "Yeah, we knew that. Let's hope we can stay out of his way. I don't need another run in with that son of a bitch."

I looked at my watch. It was after four o'clock. I hadn't heard a word from Kate. *Damn!*

"Okay," I said. "Let's wrap this up. I need to get out of here. Things to do. Tomorrow, we'll start making the rounds of the principle players, namely Dickerson and the Draycotts. Anyone have anything to add? No? Good. Bob, I want you to work with Tim. I need to know everything there is to know about Willett, Donavan and Little Jacky in particular. You can also continue to dig into the Draycotts' history. That's it. Have a good one."

They all left the office, with exception of Amanda, who remained seated, a somewhat mocking smile on her lips.

"Things to do?" she asked, as Mike closed the door behind him. "Anyone I know?"

I grinned at her. I never knew exactly what she was thinking when she spoke like that. She certainly wasn't the jealous type, although I've known her to get waspy once in a while, especially where Kate's concerned.

"Yes. I'm meeting Kate at the club, to discuss the case and... dinner."

"And for dessert? Something nice, I hope." There was no mistaking what she meant. She still wore the mocking smile, but her face had hardened. *Oh shit. Who said honesty was the best policy?*

"No, Amanda; no dessert, just dinner."

"That'll be the day." She uncrossed her legs, gifting me with a view of, well, you know, and rose from her seat. The smile was gone. "Have a good evening. You know where to find me... *if* you need me." *Sarcasm? Innuendo? What?*

"Amanda—"

"Call me tomorrow," she interrupted, and then she grabbed her iPad from my desk and walked out of the office.

Okay. That's it. I've got to figure this crap out. I have enough to cope with without having to contend with two pissed-off women. Life's too goddamn short.

I grabbed my cell and called Kate.

"Hey," I said when she answered. "I thought you were going to call me back. We going to eat or what?"

"Damn, who kicked your cat? I didn't call you back because I don't have anything yet. Yes, we're going to eat. I'll meet you at the club at seven."

"No. I'll pick you up."

"No. You won't. I need to get home before ten, and I need to drive myself. I know you. If I let you drive, it'll turn into an all-night thing. I have a full case load and I need to get some rest. I'll meet you there at seven."

"But—"

"Seven o'clock. Bye, Harry." Click. *Goddamn it. Geeze. What the hell* is *it with these women?*

I picked up the desk phone and buzzed Jacque. I asked her to call Doctor Draycott and see if she could make an appointment for me to see him the next afternoon. Then I sat back in my chair and flipped through my notes. Two minutes later, the phone buzzed and Jacque informed me that I had an appointment with both Doctors Draycott at two-fifteen tomorrow afternoon. I made note of it, gathered my stuff together, and headed home, still in a foul mood.

Chapter 7

I awoke early the following morning. No, I awoke very early, at four o'clock, and I couldn't go back to sleep. I felt lousy. I'd had too much to drink the night before, and dinner with Kate had not gone well. My fault. It must have been my conflicted interests — Kate and Amanda — but I was in a terrible mood the whole evening. Hell, I even snapped at my father, and he certainly didn't deserve it. Kate put up with my mood through an early meal and was out of there well before ten.

I went home, grabbed the bottle of Laphroaig Quarter Cask Scotch Whiskey and a glass from the bar, flopped down on the sofa, and stared out of the window. The weather had turned ugly and matched my mood perfectly. The surface the river, black and turbulent, was whipped to foam by the wind and rain that battered the glass of the floor-to-ceiling windows. When I finally turned in, it was after midnight, and three-fourths of the bottle of scotch was no more than a bleary memory. I slept fitfully until I could suffer it no more.

By seven o'clock, I'd showered, shaved, and dressed to suit my mood: black, long-sleeved dress shirt, black jeans, and black Bruno Magli Raspino boots. I scrambled some eggs, drank two cups of black coffee, climbed into my DeSantis shoulder rig, checked the Smith and Wesson M&P9, and put on a slick, black all-weather golf jacket. I looked and felt like the Grim Reaper, and it didn't make me feel any better, but what the hell. Finally, I slipped into my heavy Fjallraven Keb Hybrid Fleece coat. I might feel like shit, but I sure as hell was going to be warm doing it.

Minutes later, I was out of the condo and driving across the Thrasher Bridge in what can only be described as a monsoon. The wipers were at full speed, pounding the bulkhead, and with little effect. The rain was coming down in sheets; visibility was down to just a few yards. *Shit. I should have waited this mess out.*

It was just before eight o'clock when I pulled up outside the office parking lot. I sat and stared at the closed gates, then banged my hands on the wheel in frustration. *Damn and blast. Nobody ever closes the f... the goddamn gate. Now it's bucketing down, and they decide to play by the rules. Damn, damn, damn.*

I got out into the downpour and unlocked and opened the gates. By the time I got back into my car, I was soaked, and my mood, already as black as I thought it could possibly be, got even blacker.

By the time I'd parked the car, closed the gates — *no I didn't lock 'em, damn it* — and unlocked the side door to the office, I was in no mood for anyone. I punched up a double cup of black coffee, went to

66

my office, closed the door behind me and locked it. Then I threw off the heavy coat and settled into my chair with the coffee in hand. *I have got to sort this shit out.*

No sooner had the thought entered my head when the desk phone buzzed. *Goddamn it!*

I picked up. "Jacque. I do not want to be disturbed for the next hour. Got that?"

"Sure, Boss," Bob growled, and disconnected. I didn't give a shit.

I gave it a couple of minutes, then buzzed him back. "Sorry, Bob. What do you need?"

"Are you going visiting today? If so, I thought you might like some company."

I thought about if for a moment. "How are you progressing with the Callahan case?"

"Nothing to do now but wait. Listen, I have other things I can do."

"No," I interrupted him. "I'm going to see Dickerson. Wouldn't hurt to have some company but... what about your ankle?"

"It's a bit stiff, painful, but I can manage. I have my stick." I had to smile at that. Bob is a quiet man, but he carries a big stick (pun intended). It's usually a ball bat.

I looked at my watch. It was still only eight-forty-five. "Were you able to dig up anything on Callahan?"

"Not much. I can fill you in later."

"Okay. Give me an hour. I have some calls to make."

I grabbed my cell phone and hit the speed dial. Kate answered almost immediately.

"So," she said. "You and Amanda have a good time last night?"

"Christ, Kate. Let's not do this. I went straight home after you left. I feel lousy; I've had a lousy start to the day, and I'm heading into what promises to be a lousy morning to meet some lousy people. Happy?"

"I see. What can I do for you, Harry?" Her voice was cold, and I didn't give a shit.

"What do you have for me? I'm going to see Dickerson. I need all you have."

"You have all I have. I have two people on it. If they find anything, you'll be the first to know."

"Fine. I'll talk to you later." I hung up without bothering to say goodbye. *Shit. I'll regret that for sure.*

Chapter 8

It was a little after ten-thirty when Bob and I left the office. The ancient, two-story building that housed Blessed are the Homeless — *Wow. That's a real misnomer for sure* — stood by itself on Cherry Street, less than a half dozen blocks from my offices on Georgia. The drive, even though the rain was still coming down in buckets, took less than two minutes. I pulled into the lot at the right side of the building and parked in one of the spots marked 'Visitors'.

Looking at the old building, I had to wonder why it hadn't been torn down long ago. Seems our soon-to-be friend, Billy Dickerson, had a penchant for derelicts, edifice and human. Back in the day, before the turn of the century, it must have been a mill of some sort. Today, other than a few patches of graffiti on the front door and walls along the sidewalk, it was fairly clean, but weathered; a lonely, brick-built cube with huge windows, each one divided into nine smaller squares of glass, some of them broken. Set against an angry sky and the driving rain, surrounded by acres of concrete upon which a variety of vehicles in various states of repair sat like huge metal insects, it was a depressing pile. I shuddered to think what might be going on inside. My already dark mood turned even darker.

Fire escapes? There were none. The front door had a padlock and chain on it. *Two safety violations and we're not even inside yet.* The two other doors, one at the north side and one at the rear, were steel, locked, no handles, just bell pushes. We chose the door nearest to the car and turned our backs to the rain. Bob leaned on his stick and looked at me; I shrugged, reached out, and pushed.

A few minutes later, we heard the sounds of the locks turning and the door opened an inch or two.

"Yeah. Wadda ya want?"

"We'd like a few words with the Reverend Dickerson, please," I said, politely.

"He ain't heah." The door started to close. Bob hit it with his shoulder. It slammed back into whoever was on the other side. There was a squeal of pain. Bob pushed the heavy door and it squeaked on its hinges. It was dark inside, but not so dark we couldn't see the man on his ass on the concrete floor of the passageway.

He was rubbing his forehead. "Hey, man. What you problem is? I toll you Mr. Dickerson he ain't heah. You hurt me, man."

Bob stepped up, grabbed his arm with his free hand, and hauled him to his feet. He was young, nineteen or twenty, skinny, dressed in jeans and a T-shirt, both of which needed laundering.

70

"Lead on, Sonny," Bob said, as he let go of his arm and spun him around.

The boy staggered a couple of steps. "Lead on? Wha' you mean, lead on?"

"Take us to Mr. Dickerson, and be quick about it," I said.

"He—"

"Take us," I said, interrupting him. "If you don't, my friend here will break your arm."

That did it. He led the way to a set of concrete stairs at the far end of the passageway. They led up into a large room that was not at all what I was expecting. It covered at least two-thirds of what I assumed was the second floor, and was bright and airy. The musty smell of the lower level was absent. High ceilings had strip lights every ten feet or so. Carpet, albeit cheap, covered the floor, and was reasonably clean. A large reception desk was situated just beyond the head of the stairs. Four doors along the rear wall provided access to what I supposed must be offices. The great room was furnished with a variety of old but serviceable furniture. I counted eight sofas of one sort or another, some of them occupied by youngsters of both genders, and a half dozen coffee tables. There was a coffee station next to the reception desk.

The woman behind the desk looked to be about forty-five, and she was formidable, tall, with a nice figure, although a little on the heavy side. Her hair was dyed a weird reddish color, and hung in ringlets down her back.

"Raymond?" She looked first at the boy, then at Bob, then at me.

"They made me brung 'em up heah, Miz Dickerson." *Miz Dickerson. Must be India.*

"Mrs. Dickerson," I said, stepping forward and offering her my hand. "I'm Harry Starke, a licensed private investigator, and this is my associate, Bob Ryan."

She took my hand, squeezed gently, and then let go. "What can I do for you, Mr. Starke?"

"I'd like to have a word with your husband."

"I'm afraid that won't be possible. He's asked not to be disturbed. Would you like to make an appointment for another day?" She picked up a pen and opened a desk planner. "I have fifteen minutes open at ten o'clock on January 22."

Bob snorted, and I grinned. "Nice try, India. Tell him we're here."

"No."

I pursed my lips, nodded, looked at Bob, and nodded again. Now you have to understand that while Bob is as tall as I am — we're both six feet two

— he weighs 242 pounds to my 210. If they were looking for someone to play the Incredible Hulk, Bob would fit the bill.

He walked across the room to the first of the doors and knocked. There was no answer. He opened it and looked inside.

"What the hell do you think you're doing?" India yelled. "You can't do that. I'll call the cops."

"Fine," I said, handing her a card. "Try this number first." The card was one of Kate's. "I'm sure Lieutenant Gazzara will explain the urgency of our visit, and the need for you and Billy to cooperate."

She took the card, looked at it, and then picked up the phone and punched in a number.

"Billy," she said. "There are two private detectives out here. I think you need to see them. No, I mean right now. Yes, two of them…. No, Billy, if you don't see them, I think they will see you."

She put the phone down, smiled sweetly, and got to her feet. "Raymond," her voice was acid, "take the desk, and *don't* let anyone else in. You got that?"

The boy, obviously frightened, replaced her behind the desk, and she headed away toward the far end of the room, her hips and arms swinging as she went. She was wearing jeans and shoes with high heels. *Wow. Now that's a great ass.*

She reached the door at the far end of the room, turned the knob, pushed it open, and then stood to one side to allow us to enter.

The Reverend William Dickerson, fifty-nine years old, was a small man, not more than five feet eight inches tall. The mug shot of seven years ago did him little justice; he was, in fact, quite a handsome man. Dressed casually in a red, white, and blue checked short-sleeve shirt, baggy blue jeans with suspenders, and heavy black boots that might or might not have had steel toecaps, he looked like he'd just stepped down off a farm tractor.

His face was thinner than it was in the photo, drawn and more heavily lined. His hair was almost white, cut short, neatly trimmed. His eyes were beady and deep-set under heavily hooded white eyebrows. His nose was a little crooked. At some time in the past it must have been broken, but whoever fixed it had done a good job. His small mouth and thin lips were surrounded by a white mustache and goatee, and he had a look about him that was both benign and friendly; he looked like someone's dear old granddad. Yep, looks can be deceptive.

"Good morning, gentlemen. Good of you to drop by," he said, caustically. "Take a seat." He came around from behind his desk, waving a hand at a group of five comfortable chairs. "India, tell Darius to get in here." She nodded, left the room, and closed the door behind her.

"Now, what the hell do you two want?" he asked, angrily. "You ain't the cops. I don't have to talk to you."

Bob and I sat, and Dickerson did, too, facing us.

"We're here to talk to you about Hill House," I said.

His jaw dropped, he screwed up his eyes, and leaned forward in his chair, his elbows on his knees. "Whaaat? Hill House? That was more than ten years ago. It was a dump. I thought they'd pulled it down."

"Soon, Mr. Dickerson, soon. What were you doing there in those days?"

"The same as we're doing here. We provide shelter, along with medical and spiritual support for the homeless...."

He was interrupted by a knock at the door.

"Come in, Darius."

The door opened and a man walked in. He was black, handsome, about six feet tall, well-built, about thirty years old. His narrow face was accented by a thin mustache and a small goatee; his hair was cropped close. He was wearing a dark gray hoodie, jeans and Air Jordans.

"This is one of my assistants, Darius Willett," Dickerson said. "He helps to keep order around here. Sit down, Darius."

He did. He flopped down next to Dickerson, slouched, his long legs stretched out in front of him, his elbows on the arms of the chair, and fingers steepled together. He glared at me over the top of them.

I looked at Bob. He'd caught it, too, and he gave me a slight nod. I was not the only one to notice the bulge under Willett's hoodie; the man was carrying. *Time for shock and awe, I think. Set the tone for the interview.*

I put my hands on the arms of the chair, pushed up onto my feet, and took a step forward. He didn't even see it coming. I swept my hand up under my jacket, pulled the M&P9, and jammed it up under his nose. It happened so quickly he took an involuntary gulp of air, threw his arms in the air, and jerked his head back against the chair. *Geeze, don't his nose look funny all scrunched up like that?*

It was a serious moment, and the stupid thought was uncalled for, but hey, that's me.

"What the hell?" Dickerson yelled, as he jumped to his feet.

"Sit down and stay calm, both of you," I said, reaching up under Willett's hoodie and relieving him of the .45 Colt M1911 semi-automatic.

I stepped back, holstered the nine, ejected the clip from the .45, worked the action, and ejected the cartridge from the chamber, stripped the clip, and threw the shells into a flowerpot on the table. The gun had been loaded with hollow-points; nasty. I tossed the firearm onto Willett's lap. The heavy weapon landed hard on his package, causing him to gasp.

"Now, Mr... oh, sorry. That should be *Reverend* Dickerson," I said, as I returned to my seat. "I feel a little more comfortable knowing I'm not going to have to kill your boy; at least I hope I'm not."

I looked sideways at Bob; he was smiling, but there was no humor in it. His own jacket was open, revealing the Glock .380 on his belt.

Darius Willett was now sitting upright, holding the empty firearm in one hand and nursing his jewels with the other. The look on his face would have shriveled lesser men, which Bob and I were not.

"You're one crazy son of a bitch," he growled at me. "I should bust your ass for that."

I grinned at him.

"Who are these two assholes, Billy?" Willett asked. His voice was strained. He obviously wasn't used to being on the receiving end.

Billy? More an equal than assistant, I think.

"They're private cops; want to talk about Hill House, and you're right: he is a crazy son of a bitch. You pull a stunt like that again, Starke, and I'll have you arrested."

Willett's eyes had narrowed, his forehead ridged with frown lines. "Say whut? Hill House? That ol' dump on McCallie? Whut you wanna know 'bout that foh?"

I ignored him (so did his boss) and directed my attention to Dickerson.

"You ran a business in Hill House for a number of years," I said, "from sometime in 1998 until you were thrown out in June of 2005. What was that all about?"

"I don't know what business it is of yours, or why I should even talk to you, but I ran the house as a charity, a homeless shelter, and I wasn't thrown out. I had a good offer and I moved out. Darius, here, was one of my rescues. He's been with me ever since."

"Mostly young girls, right?" Bob said.

Dickerson said nothing.

"Young girls?" Bob asked again.

78

"Some were girls, yes." His eyes were shifting. It seemed he wouldn't look at either one of us.

"And what happened to them, the *young* girls?" Bob is nothing if not persistent.

"What do you mean, *what happened to them?* Some we found homes for, some were returned to their parents, and some ran away again. I don't like these questions. What's this all about, Mr. Starke?"

"How many girls, over the years, did you find homes for?" I asked.

"Hell, I don't know. You'll have to ask India. She keeps track of things like that, not me."

"Okay, I can do that. So tell me, how many young people do you have here now?"

"Including staff...." He thought for a moment, his lips moving, counting to himself, then said, "Thirty-seven, plus India and me."

"Tell us about your criminal record," Bob said.

"Whaaat? What? The hell with you," he spluttered, and started to get to his feet. "Get the hell out of here."

"*Mr.* Dickerson," I said, quietly. "Please sit down. You were arrested six times for pimping between 1986 and 2008.... Hold on. Let me finish," I said, as he opened his mouth to interrupt. "Never once did you do time for it. Much of that time, you were at Hill House providing *shelter* for young girls

79

and boys. How many of them, I wonder, did you put on the streets? Now you're at it again, running another shelter, and again it's mostly for young girls. Must be profitable. You know what I think? I think you have someone important in your pocket. Who are you paying off, Billy?"

"Screw you, Starke. You've no idea what you're talking about. I run a legitimate 501c3, non-profit charitable home here. I do good work. God's work. Good community work. Now, if you're finished, get the hell out of my office."

"Billy," I said. "Listen to me. The reason we're here is because they found the body of a teenage girl under the floorboards of what was the master bedroom of that house. It's been there since you ran the place." *Not quite a lie, but let's see what he thinks of it.*

He stared at me, his eyes wide, his mouth open. "What are you talking about?" he stammered.

"A young black girl, aged about seventeen, stuffed under the boards ten or twelve years ago, when you were in residence. Any thoughts, Billy?"

He looked furtively at Willett, got no reaction from him, and turned his stare again at me. "I dunno what you're talking about. That was the communal room back then, like out there." He waved his hand in the direction of the door. "I don't know nothin' about no body, or no girl. Nothin'."

I looked at Willett. He stared back at me, his eyes mere slits, unblinking. The muscles of his face were tight, but twitching, like he had a tick. I looked again at Dickerson.

"Why do you allow your *assistant* to carry a concealed weapon?" I asked. "You claim to be a pastor. Why would he need one?"

"Do you know this area, *at all*, Starke? It's a goddamn jungle out there: street gangs, illegals. Darius, and a couple of others, looks after security around here. A gun is a necessity. I have one. Hell, even India has one."

He was right. It was a rough neighborhood. By now though, I was convinced of two things: one, this man was no reverend; he was still a pimp, and two, I wasn't going to get a whole lot more out of him, except....

"What's your connection with Salvatore De Luca, Billy?"

He looked stunned; the color emptied from his face. Out of the corner of my eye, I saw that Willett had also stiffened.

"Who? I don't know anybody by that name."

"Sure you do. Everybody knows Sal. Just the fact that you deny knowing him tells me that you do know him. You're one shady son of a bitch, Billy, and I'm not finished with you yet, not by a long shot. I'll be back. Bob, let's get out of this... this septic tank."

I got to my feet and walked out of his office into the big room beyond. The air out there was like a breath of spring... nah, it was just better than in Billy's office, but it was still a swamp. Bob followed me down the stairs and out into the parking lot and the rain.

"Goddamn it. Look at that." Oh I was pissed. Someone had taken something sharp to the Maxima, and it wasn't something small, like a key. The two deep, wide scratches, one along each side, and two huge crosses, one on the trunk and one on the hood, would need a full paint job to repair. *Christ. Sons of bitches.*

I drove the car the few blocks back to my offices and called the dealership and had them come pick it up. Then I called a rental company and booked a car for the next couple of weeks. *Thank the Lord for insurance companies.*

Chapter 9

"So, what do you think?" I asked Bob as we sat together in my office.

"Of the Reverend Dickerson? He's one nasty son of a bitch. He's into trafficking. I'd bet my last dollar on it. The kid under the floor was one of his victims; I'd bet on that, as well."

I nodded. "Those were my thoughts, too. I don't know about the body, though. We need to identify her before we can even hope to figure anything out."

Bob said nothing. He stared down into the steam from his coffee cup. "What's next, Harry?"

"Well, if you'll drive, we'll get some lunch, and then go see the Draycotts. I have an appointment for two-fifteen. When we've finished there, you can take me to the rental company to pick up a car. What do you want to eat for lunch?"

Well, hell, he wanted Mexican. Now I like the real thing, in Mexico, but here in Chattanooga not so much. We settled on Chinese at the Forbidden City on Gunbarrel Road.

We ate, for the most part, in silence; mostly that was my fault. Bob knows me well, perhaps too well, and he could see I needed to think. My appetite was away with the birds. I picked and played with my spicy chicken, then pushed it away, sipped on my iced tea, and stared out of the window at the rain, but that was not what I saw. In my imagination, I watched the scene, some ten years ago, as I thought it might have played out; the young girl struggling for her life, a fight she was doomed to lose. I tried to shake it off, but couldn't. It did my already black mood no good and, for a moment, I wondered if I should call it a day and go home. I didn't, but I knew I'd need to be very careful during the upcoming interview with the Draycotts. These people were not the Dickersons.

"Ready, Bob?" I asked, as he laid down his fork. He nodded. I dropped two twenties on the table and got to my feet.

Outside, the weather was even worse. Thunder and lightning crackled overhead. The driving rain gusted and swirled between the streets. The roads were fast-running creeks, and the drains were barely able to cope with the volume. It was beyond depressing: just what I needed.

We were already on Gunbarrel, so the drive to the Draycotts' place on East Brainerd Road took less than five minutes.

The Clermont complex was actually located just off East Brainerd Road. For some reason, maybe it was just the crappy weather, the large, three-story, brick-built block of living units, surrounded as it was by a high brick wall complete with electronic gates, reminded me of the county jail. *That's not a good start.*

Bob pulled the car up to the electronic key pad and hit the buzzer. A tinny, almost incoherent voice asked, "Can I help you?"

Bob told the little box who we were, and a moment later the gate swung slowly open.

The main building was quite new: a large rectangular block built with beige-colored bricks and a flat roof, surrounded by neatly landscaped gardens. The windows, three rows, one atop the other, were small, which only added to the prison-like facade. A circular drive took us to the front door where a young woman in an open lab coat was waiting at the top of the five steps.

She introduced herself as Bonnie Parsons, the receptionist, and showed us through into a large, airy waiting room.

"Doctor Draycott will be with you shortly," she said, leaving us alone. I looked around the room: nice, comfortable furniture, typical of a doctor's waiting room. The walls were covered with framed photographs. Many of them were of young people, some were obviously of the Draycotts. Several of the photos were of particular interest: group photos; some of them obviously taken during the time when the Draycotts were at Hill House. Two of them included a much younger William and India Dickerson and two other adults I assumed were the Draycotts. A third photo included only the four of them, and the man I assumed was Draycott had his arm around Dickerson's shoulder. Both men had big smiles on their faces. I beckoned Bob over and pointed them out. He looked carefully at them, then at me, his eyes wide.

"Wow," he mouthed.

I nodded.

"Looking into my past, are you? Good times, those. I'm Sam Draycott," he said, walking toward us with his hand out, "and one of you must be Mr. Starke."

"I am," I said, taking his hand and shaking it. His grip was firm. "And this is my associate, Bob Ryan."

"Nice to meet you both. Why don't we go through to my office? Would you like coffee, tea, water?" We didn't, and he led the way along a pristine corridor any hospital would have been proud of to an already open door.

"Please, sit down." He indicated a group of four chairs around a low, but very large coffee table. "Are you sure you wouldn't like some coffee? Doctor

Draycott will join us shortly." *Doctor Draycott... I thought... oh hell, yes. There are two of them.*

Draycott was an impressive personage, about as different from Billy Dickerson as it was possible to get. At sixty-two years old, and almost six feet tall, he was fit, gray haired, and wore a classic Van Dyke beard. His crisp, white shirt was accented by a pale blue tie. The tan pants were sharply creased, and the wide leather belt sported an incongruously large silver buckle. Over it all, he wore an open lab coat. Impressive.

Again, we declined his offer, and sat down, Bob and I on one side of the table, Draycott on the other.

"I'm sorry. I hope I haven't kept you waiting," Mrs. Draycott said as she entered.

The black business suit fit her perfectly; the perfect contrast for her bobbed, platinum blonde hair. The skirt was cut three inches above the knee and her calves were accentuated by the five-inch heels she was wearing. We all stood. I made the introductions. In those high heels, she was the taller of the two Draycotts. The greeting over with, she joined her husband at the far side of the table and sat down. She was wearing glasses with large frames. She removed them, laid them down on the table, crossed her legs at the ankles, and clasped her hands together on her knees.

I knew she was sixteen years Draycott's junior, but she looked older than her forty-six years. It was easy to see that although her body had weathered the years well, she'd had some work done on her face; her skin was smooth and blemish-free, but stretched a little too tightly, especially at the corners of her eyes, and her lips were just a little fuller than was natural. Even so, she was a very attractive woman. Her demeanor, however, was austere, even a little hostile.

"I presume this is about Hill House; the body that was found under the floor?" Sam Draycott said. "I have already spoken to the police, a Lieutenant Gazzara. She said you would be getting in touch, and she asked us to cooperate. We are pleased to do so. So, please, ask your questions, Mr. Starke. We'll do our best to answer them."

"Thank you, Doctor, but if you don't mind, I'd like to get a handle on what you do *here*, just the background stuff, of course."

"Yes, why not." He glanced sideways at his wife as he said it. Nothing. *Hmmm. This one is hard to read.*

"I'll try to be brief. The Clermont Foundation is a 501c3 nonprofit organization. We provide emergency shelter, transitional housing, medical and support services, and education to homeless girls aged between twelve and twenty-one, both here in the city and in Hamilton Country. We offer our services in the belief that youth must have their basic needs met before they can begin to build a promising future for themselves."

"Those needs," I said, "would be extensive, correct?"

"Indeed they would, and we provide for all of their needs: medical, which is my department, mine and my staff. The mental side of things is handled by Ellen and her staff; she is a psychiatrist. We provide clean, comfortable housing for them, here in this block, which has a variety of communal and recreation areas. There are also four separate quadraplexes on the grounds: independent living for those girls who can handle it. It's a fairly substantial operation. We can look after up to sixty girls here."

"I understand the principle, Dr. Draycott, but why just young girls? Why not cater to the homeless in general, and why no boys?"

"Please, call me Sam. To answer the first part of your question, I, that is we," he looked at his wife, "decided a long time ago that it would be better to devote our limited resources to the most vulnerable section of the homeless community, young girls. As to males... well... it just isn't practical to mix the genders, if you understand me."

I nodded. I certainly did understand.

"Tell me about the girls, Doctor, if you don't mind. Where do they come from? How do you find them?"

"Most of them are runaways," Ellen Draycott said. "Some are victims of trafficking. Some we pick up off the streets. We have a team, well, just two people, who do nothing but travel the streets looking for them, and a nasty job it is, too. Others are referred to us by DCS and by local churches. Unfortunately, we can take only the neediest cases; money is a big factor."

"I see...." I said. I must have looked skeptical, because she interrupted me.

"Mr. Starke. What do you think happens to a young girl who has been locked out by her family, or who flees to escape an abusive home situation? What about those girls in foster care? What becomes of them when they age out of that program? Those girls are not prepared to take their place in society. Most are not properly educated. Most can't get a job. Just imagine waking up on your eighteenth birthday and finding yourself homeless, jobless, and alone. Do we simply ignore them, turn them loose and let them fall by the wayside? I should think not."

"You paint a vivid and terrifying picture, Doctor," I said.

"Not vivid or terrifying enough, I'm afraid. Ex-foster care children, most of them, are not mature enough to be called adults even if technically they are. And they are certainly not the biggest problem. Imagine trying to save a fifteen-year-old runaway turned hooker. Most of them... no, all of them, are tied to pimps, scared shitless — please excuse the language — of what will happen to them if they are disloyal. It can be done, but it's not easy, is it, Sam?"

He heaved a sigh and shook his head. "No, it isn't, but we do what we can. We offer supervised group living that provides housing for the girls while they finish high school. They work here or in approved sponsored employment ten to twenty hours per week. They keep sixty-five percent of their earnings, which is banked for them and they receive training in money management in the hopes that they can make the transition to self-sufficiency. They are taught independent living skills, training on topics such as financial literacy, household maintenance, and health education. As they progress toward economic independence, they begin to pay rent, which increases progressively until they are fully self-sufficient.

"We have room for thirty participants here in the main building where we can provide a fully supervised, home-like environment. We also have the four on-site locations, each one can house up to eight girls. I wish we had more room, but... well, we just don't have the money."

"How long do the girls stay with you?" I asked.

"Typically," Ellen said, "the girls enter the program through our Emergency Shelter, and then, if we can't reunite them with their families, they transfer into the supervised group living program. From that point on, they are provided with individual, wraparound case management, educational support, counseling, medical treatment, therapeutic recreation, and employment. A girl might be in the program for as long as nine years, or as short as six months. There is no set path to rehabilitation, but when they leave here, they will, we hope, have become responsible and productive members of society, well able to support themselves. We are very proud of what we do here, and of our achievements."

"So, Doctor," I said, not directly to either one of them, "just how big of a problem are we talking about? I ask, because I think it ties in with what we want to talk to you about."

Ellen wrinkled her nose, then said, "Chattanooga is no different than any other city, small or large. For every child we have in our care, there are at least five more still on the streets."

I shook my head. I knew it was bad, but I had no idea *how* bad. I wondered if anyone really did.

"That's... depressing," I said. "I know you're both very busy, so I'll get to the reason for our visit. Let's talk about Hill House. You still own it, correct?"

"Well, yes," Sam Draycott said, "but it's scheduled for demolition, as soon as the police release it, so I'm told."

"That, I'm afraid, may not be anytime soon. The crime scene unit still has it, and it's unlikely they will release it until it's been cleared; it's a big house."

He nodded, but said nothing. Doctor Ellen sat with her hands clasped together in her lap; she also had nothing to say.

I flipped the lock screen on my iPad and opened the file.

"You were in residence there from June 2005 until August of 2008, a little more than three years, correct?"

They both nodded.

"And I assume you were doing the same there as here?"

Again, they both nodded. "On a much smaller scale, of course," Doctor Ellen said. "We were not able to take more than sixteen, seventeen girls at the most."

"Now," I said. "I know it was a long time ago, but did you lose any of the girls? Did any of them go missing?"

"Yes, of course," Sam said. "That's a huge problem, even here. There are always runaways; most of them return to their pimps. Some, we just lose track of."

"Do you keep records of your losses, and if you do, do you still have those for the time when you were at Hill House?"

"Of course we do, but we don't call them losses," Ellen said. "They are failures; failures on our part. We failed those girls. We are computerized now, but we still have the old paper files. We can let you look at them, here. I'm not going to ask for a court order. I know you can get one, but they are confidential, even those of the girls who went missing. What period are we talking about?"

"I'd like to look at the files for 2005 through 2008, just those who went missing for now. I may need to look at those of the rest of your charges during that period later."

She rose to her feet. "Please, give me a moment. I'll have them located for you."

She was gone for no more than a couple of minutes. "Bonnie will find them, but it will take a few minutes." She resumed her seat.

"How well do you remember your charges from those days?" I asked.

"Why, I remember them all, vividly," Doctor Sam said.

Doctor Ellen merely nodded her agreement.

"The girl found under the floor was African-America. She would have been around seventeen, give or take a year. Do you remember anyone like that?"

"I do," Ellen said. "In fact I remember a great many, but only a handful of them went missing: five or six, maybe. One young lady came to see me just a couple of weeks ago. We try to maintain contract with all of our girls, but it's not easy. Some, though, do like to keep in touch with us, don't they, Sam?"

"Would it be possible for me to talk to her, do you think?" I asked.

"It might," she said, "but I would need to check with her before I gave you her contact information. I'll do that and let you know."

"Thank you, Doctor," I said. "Now. I'd to talk to you about the Reverend Dickerson."

That brought a smile to Sam's face. "*Reverend?* When did that happen?"

"I have no clue," I said. "I don't even know if it's an official title. How well did you know him?"

"I didn't. Well, I did, but we met only a couple of times. It was just before we took over Hill House."

"You weren't friends?"

"Good God, no! The man is a low life; his wife is no better. It's to them you should be directing your attention, right, Ellen?"

She nodded. "It was always my belief that their intentions toward the girls were less than honorable. I'll go further: I think he's a procurer, a pimp."

"Those are strong words, Doctor," I said. "Do you have anything to back them up?"

"Other than my gut feelings, no, but I know people, Mr. Starke, and he represents the worst of the worst. I pity any girl who falls into his clutches. I wish to God we, that is Chattanooga, could be rid of him."

The door opened and the receptionist came in carrying a small stack of files. She placed them on the table in front of Doctor Ellen, who uncrossed her feet, leaned forward, and picked them up.

"Thank you, Bonnie," she said. "That will be all for now."

I counted the files as she leafed through them. There were nine.

"You can look at them," she said, replacing them on the table, "but I can't allow you to take notes or to photograph them. Now, if you don't mind, I have an appointment. Have you finished with us?"

"Bob." I looked at him. "Do you have anything?" He merely shook his head.

"Yes, Doctor," I said. "That will be all for now, but I may need to talk to you again, if you don't mind."

I closed my iPad, rose from the chair, shook hands with the two doctors, and followed Ellen out of the room. She took us to a small conference room and placed the files on the table, and then she picked up the phone, hit the buzzer, and said, "Bonnie. Will you come to the conference room, please?"

Bonnie arrived a few seconds later and Ellen gave her instructions: she was to watch us: no notes, no photos, and then she left, her high heels clicking away along the corridor.

I flipped quickly though the files, discarding those that didn't fit the profile. I was left with three that did: one African-American girl aged eighteen, and two mixed-race girls, one eighteen and one nineteen.

I looked quickly through the file of the black girl, made mental notes, and then handed it off to Bob. I did the same with other two files, again making metal notes of the names, ages, and general

97

descriptions. I don't have eidetic memory, but what I do have is better than most.

I looked at Bob. "Ready?"

He nodded, stacked the files neatly, and pushed the pile toward Bonnie, who was smiling apologetically.

"Thank you, Bonnie," I said. "We'll be going now."

"Did you get it?" I asked as Bob slid into the driver's seat a few moments later.

He grinned at me. "What do you think? I recorded the whole damn interview, and every page of the three files. I also have the visit with the Dickersons." He waved his right hand at me, exposing the watch on his wrist.

I have one just like it, although mine is more sophisticated than his, complements of the Secret Service and Senator Linda Michaels. It's a fully functioning wristwatch, with a few high-tech extras, including video and audio transmission. The range is about a half mile, more than enough to reach the receiver unit and its digital recorder in the trunk of Bob's car. It's one of those expensive little toys that more than pays for itself, as it did today.

"So," I said. "What did you think of them?"

Bob is one astute son of a bitch. He can read people like no one I ever met. I trust his judgement, implicitly.

"Well, I tell ya, Harry. I don't like either one of 'em. They were way too smooth. Couple of high-class snakes, if you ask me. He couldn't look at either one of us, an' I get the feelin' she's a cold fish. Sophisticated, both of them, and obviously good at what they do, and they seem to have a genuine affinity for their work, but they weren't completely forthcoming. Both of 'em were guarded, careful with their answers. I don't like 'em."

"Yep, I noticed it, too, especially when I asked about the Dickersons. He was obviously lying. He's knows them better than he cares to admit. That photo on the wall of the waiting room proves that. By the way, did you get pics of the photos?" *Stupid question. Of course he did.*

He didn't bother to answer. He just turned his head and gave me a big grin.

Back at the office, he parked the car, retrieved the digital unit from the trunk, handed it to me, leaned heavily on his cane, and limped painfully into the office. I handed the unit to Tim, told him what I needed, and signaled Bob to join me. Together, we sat back and enjoyed a large measure of Laphroaig scotch whiskey, ice only, no water. It had been a good day, even though it was still raining hard. Then I had a thought.

"Oh shit, Bob. We forgot to go to the rental company." I looked at the glass in my hand. It was empty. "Damn it. Can't go now."

"Hey, man. I'm sorry. It completely slipped my mind."

"No worries. I'll think of something. If not, I'll sleep here, on the couch. It wouldn't be the first time."

Chapter 10

It was after six when they all finally left the office and I was alone. I'd had just one more large Laphroaig and was feeling no pain. I looked at my watch: six-fifteen. *Hell, she's still on the set. Oh, what the hell.*

I hit the speed dial on my iPhone. "This is Amanda. Please leave a message." I hung up. *Damn it.*

I poured another Laphroaig, just a small one. Well, maybe not so small. Damn it, I was hungry. *I know. I'll order pizza.*

No sooner had I done so than my iPhone rang.

"Harry, you called. What's up?"

"Hello, Amanda. Nothing now; I fixed it."

"Fixed what? What's wrong?"

"I told you, nothing. My car's in the shop. Some asshole did a number on it with a screwdriver and I have no transport. I thought you might have liked to pick me and we could have gotten something to eat. That's all."

"Where are you, Harry?"

"At the office, but...." *She hung up! Damn it, Amanda. I hate it when you do that.*

She arrived some thirty minutes later. I had already unlocked the door for her, and the gates to the lot. She was bundled up like a damn Eskimo. A huge, white, knee-length parka, white leather gloves, a huge wooly hat that covered her ears, and big rubber boots. I don't know whether it was the Laphroaig or what — I was by now certainly three sheets in the wind — but when I saw her come clumping in the door to my office, I burst out laughing.

"Screw you, Harry Starke."

"Yes, please," I said, "but have some pizza first and there's some wine in the fridge; white and red, help yourself."

I leaned back in the big chair and watched as she divested herself of her outer layers. *Oh my God. She is one of the most beautiful women I have ever seen.*

The weather outside was dreadful, about as bad as it ever gets in Chattanooga, except for when it snows, but underneath all of the outer layers, she was dressed for summer. She was wearing a powder blue, woolen dress, so thin and light you could almost see through it. What she had on under that I had no idea, but I had a feeling I would soon find out.

Again, I don't know if it was the effect of the drink, but there are times when I'm with Amanda that I think I'm in love; this was one of them. She's a very rare breed. She knows who and what I am and puts up with my catting around, not that I do very

102

much of that anymore, not since she and I became an item, that is, but once in a while.... Well, you know.

"Harry. You're drunk. What the hell happened?"

"Drunk, my dear? How can you say that? Wasn't it Dean Martin that said, 'You're not drunk if you can lie on the floor without holding on?'" I stood up, held my arms wide. "See?" I said. "No hands."

She smiled, and began to turn.

"Wait," I said. She waited. I took a step forward and wrapped my arms around her. How the hell she managed to hold me up, I don't know.

"Damn it, Harry," she giggled. "You *are* drunk. Back off. Sit down. I need the bathroom and I need something to drink. I'll be back." *I'll be back? Who was it said that? Ronald something. Or was it Harold? Couldn't have been. Hell, I'm Harold. Screw it. Somebody said it. Eh, who cares?*

"Harry? *Harry!*"

"What?"

"Wake up, you ass. I've only been gone a minute."

I grinned up at her. "Me, too, honey."

I think I began to sober up around nine o'clock that night. I remember Amanda was watching the tail end of O'Reilly on Fox, and that I was as thirsty as the devil. She looked round at me, obviously disgusted.

"Go get a shower, you ass, and change clothes. You stink."

Fortunately, I was able to do just that. I have a full bathroom next to my office, and I keep several changes of clothes in the closet.

She was right. I did need the shower. I turned up the heat. The water was so hot it all but blistered my skin, but it worked. Ten minutes later, I was new man.

"Hey," I said, as I walked back into my office. "Did you leave me any pizza? I'm starving." Again, I was struck by how beautiful this woman was. Even after a full day's work, she was stunning.

"Yes. I put some out for you, and some coffee. No more booze, please?"

I nodded. "No more. I promise."

I had barely swallowed my first mouthful when my cell phone rang. I looked at the screen, but didn't recognize the number. I thumbed the lock and took the call.

"Harry Starke."

"Harry. It's Benny."

Benny? Benny... oh, okay.

"Benny Hinkle?"

"Yeah, that Benny." *Sarcasm. Not like Benny.*

Benny Hinkle is a weird character. He owns and runs a downtown bar, the Sorbonne, a nightclub. It's a dark, sleazy cavern inhabited by Chattanooga's night crawlers, weirdos and freaks, and by many members of the underworld and, at times... by me, though I don't frequent it quite as often as I once did. Benny's a strange little worm, a fat little bastard, bald; an unctuous, unkempt slob with a penchant for making money. He's a night crawler, a fat little vampire who ventures out of the depths of his cave at the rear of the tavern only after sundown, to suck the money from a gullible younger generation via watered booze and food of questionable age. *And he's calling me?*

"What do you want, Benny?"

"I have a nugger of information you might be interested in."

"Nugger? Don't you mean nugget?"

"Whatever. Do you want it or not?"

"Depends on what it's going to cost me, and how important it might be."

"Oh, it's important, and it's not gonna cost you a nickel. I had a friend of yours in here a few minutes ago, Tony Carpeta."

"Carpeta? What did he want?"

"He wanted you, Harry. Wanted to know if I'd seen you lately."

"Did he say why?"

"Nope, but he looked mean and he wasn't alone. He's found a new partner since you offed Gino. Some big Mexican dude. Goes by the name of Jesus. Nasty-lookin' bastard. Tony gave me a number to call if you was to come in."

"Hmmm. Why are you telling me this, Benny? It's not like I'm your soul mate." *Oh god. Did I really just say that?"*

"I dunno. Figured you'd owe me one, is all. Now you do, right?"

"Depends on what you figure the tally might be, but yeah, I owe you one. Thanks."

"Yeah, same to ya. I'm already regrettin' it. I just know it's gonna come back to haunt me. Bye, Harry. I'll be in touch." He disconnected, leaving me with the phone still at my ear, staring at the remains of the pizza.

"Harry," Amanda said. "I heard some of that. I heard the name Carpeta. What was it about?"

Tony Carpeta. That means Sal De Luca. That's not good.

"Nothing for you to worry your sweet head about. It seems that Sal is looking for me."

106

She clapped her hand to her mouth and gasped. "Oh my God. That's awful. What does he want?"

"No idea. Well, yeah, I do. I went to see the Dickersons today, and during the conversation, Sal's name came up. I brought it up. It wasn't well received, to say the least."

Salvatore 'Sal' De Luca runs a small, but exclusive Italian restaurant just off Market Street. He'd like you to think it was his primary business, but it's not. Sal is a 'made man,' a mobster with connections both in New York and Miami. I've known him for quite a while, and it had been less than four months ago I caused him a lot of aggravation. I'd broken his finger and I'd killed one of his boys, Gino Polti, right there in the restaurant. Polti and Carpeta were two of his soldiers; Carpeta still is.

So Dickerson called Sal, did he? That tells me something; shit, it tells me a lot. Oh hell. I really don't need this kind of trouble; not again. Maybe I should go see him. Sheesh. Maybe I shouldn't.

But I knew I would.

I filled Amanda in on the events of the day, and then we watched TV, well, for a while. We argued about going home. I wanted to stay, but she didn't think that was a good idea. I had no car and wasn't fit to drive anyway, so I left it up to her. She took me home to my place, which, so it turned out, was absolutely the right choice.

Chapter 11

The following morning, Thursday, Mike came by at eight o'clock to pick me up. He dropped me off at the car rental and then headed back to the office. It took all of thirty minutes to rent a black Ford Explorer, but by nine o'clock I was in my office drinking a large cup of Italian Dark Roast. I love those quiet moments. Unfortunately, they never last for long; today was no exception.

Kate arrived, with Lonnie Guest in tow, only a few minutes after I did. Jacque showed them in, and I had them both sit. Lonnie was his usual supercilious self, something I was slowly but surely getting used to, not by choice, but because he was now officially Kate's partner, had been for almost a year. *Poor Kate!*

I looked first at Kate, then at Lonnie. "You guys want coffee?"

Lonnie did; Kate didn't. I went and got it for him, black, no sugar. *I can't believe I did that.*

"So what's new?" I asked, as I returned to my chair behind the desk.

"Nothing," Kate said, "which is why we're here. Where are you with your investigation?"

"Well, Bob and I went visiting yesterday: the Dickersons and the Draycotts." I gave them the short version of what we learned at the Clermont

Foundation first. When I'd finished, Kate asked for my impressions.

"It's hard to say. They seem sincere in what they're doing," I said, "but they're a strange couple. Both Bob and I feel they're hiding something. They're just a tad too slick: very professional, but... well, she comes across as a hard ass, and I'd say she's very much in charge of the operation. We also asked them what they knew about the Dickersons. Their first reaction was that they didn't know them, but... hold on a minute."

I picked up the phone and buzzed Tim.

"Hey," I said. "Do you have those photos downloaded from the recorder yet? Good. I need copies. In here. Soon as you can."

I barely had time to put the phone down when the there was a knock at the door and Tim walked in. He handed me a sheaf of eight by ten color prints. He'd done a good job. There were more than a dozen of them taken on the wall of the Draycotts' waiting room. Some were a bit fuzzy, but all were recognizable. I flipped through them, looking for one in particular. I found it, stared at it, and smiled to myself. It was fuzzy all right, but they were easily recognizable: Sam Draycott had his arm around Billy Dickerson's shoulder.

"Looks like they knew each other quite well, wouldn't you say?" I asked as I flipped the print across the desk to Kate.

"Oh yeah," she said. "Those two know each other. So, do you think there's something going on between them?"

"As I said, it's hard to tell at this point. We don't know enough about either of them, although Sam Draycott seemed more than a little contemptuous when he spoke of them: called them 'lowlifes,' as I recall."

"Can I get a copy of this?" she asked as she laid the print on my desk.

"Yes, of course, and the rest of them, and, I hope, copies of the files of three missing girls who disappeared during the period from 2004 to 2008. Bob managed to photograph those, too. There were nine in all, but six of them were Caucasian, so we discounted them. The three we copied? Hell, I don't know. From the quick glance I had of them, they are all a bit iffy, but we'll know soon enough."

"So, what about the Dickersons?" she asked.

"That's a whole 'nother story. That place on Cherry is a swamp. The Dickersons, well, he's a piece of work. Her, we didn't see much of but she's obviously a hard ass, too."

I gave them the rundown on that visit, too, including what had happened to my car.

"So, what do you think is going on there?" Lonnie spoke for the first time.

"I think Blessed are the Homeless is a gateway," I said. "I think they're into trafficking, girls, and maybe boys. It's a full-scale operation; he's even got a bunch of armed thugs on the property. Might be worth a visit by your people, to check gun permits. His assistant, Darius Willett, was toting a Colt .45 semi-automatic. I know it's a rough area, but a cannon like that? Well, you know."

"Might be worth a quick visit," she said. "What do you think, Lonnie?"

He grinned at her. "Today?" And he was just the man for the job.

"No time today," she said. "Later, maybe."

"One more thing," I said. "I asked him about Sal De Luca. It wasn't well received. He said he didn't know him, but I know damn well that he does. In fact, I'd be willing to bet that they're partners. We know that Sal's been a major player in local prostitution for years; it makes sense."

"That's not good, Harry," she said. "There's a lot of bad blood between you and De Luca. You can't go fooling around with him again; remember what happened last time. You got real lucky."

112

"The hell I can't," I said. "He's already involved. I had a call from Benny Hinkle last night. Apparently De Luca's goons were in the Sorbonne yesterday, and they were looking for me. I can't let that go. I have to know what he's up to."

"So," she said. "You're going after him?"

"I'm going to see him. I have to. If I don't... I just have to, that's all."

She nodded. "Okay. If you must, you must, but I don't like it. You want me and Lonnie to go with you?"

I thought about it for a minute. It was tempting, but I didn't want to show weakness. I had to do this thing alone.

"Thanks for the offer," I said, "but no. This is between him and me. If I can sort it out, I will. If not...."

"Shit, Harry." She shook her head, frustrated, worried, I could tell, and there was good reason to be. Sal De Luca was bad news. He was an evil son of a bitch, and he held a grudge. He owed me one, big time.

"When?" she asked.

"This afternoon, early. Two o'clock."

"We'll be there. Oh, stop it," she interrupted as I was about to protest. "We'll be outside. If anything bad happens, and you need us, the response time will be zero. That's it. No arguments." So I didn't argue. I just sat back in my chair and grinned at her.

"Have you guys had any luck finding out who she is?" Kate asked, changing the subject. "The girl, the body?" she explained, when she saw I wasn't with her.

"Oh, no. Other than the three files from the Draycotts, that is. Hold on. I'll make a call."

I punched the number for the Forensic Center into my cell. Doc Sheddon answered himself.

"Hey, Doc. Is Carol busy?"

"Hold on. I'll get her."

"Hey, Carol," I said, when she picked up. "How is the cast of the skull coming along?"

"Already done. I have two in fact."

"Fantastic. If you don't mind, I'll send Mike over for one. He'll be there in twenty. Is that okay?"

She said that it was. I thanked her and disconnected. I punched the intercom button and gave Mike his instructions, then I buzzed Tim and asked him to come in.

"Take a seat, Tim." He did, his eyebrows raised in question.

"You said you had a friend at UT who needs a project. I have one. Can you get him in here?"

"It's a she, Samantha, and yes. How soon?"

"Right away. An hour?"

"Damn, Mr. Starke," he said. "You don't ask for much. I'll call her. See what I can do."

"Good. Thank you. Now, what about the missing persons data banks? Have you been able to find anything?"

"I have six hits that sort of match the little bit we have: broken wrist, etc., but I'm still looking. I hope to have more by the end of the day."

"Okay, fine. I've just sent Mike over to the Forensic Center. Carol has a cast of the girl's skull for you. As soon as Samantha gets here, let me know. Okay?"

He nodded, got up, left the room, and closed the door behind him.

"Well," I said to Kate. "That will save the city a nice piece of change. If I can, I'll have her do the work here. I have a spare office she can use."

"So," Kate said. "You think it's going to work?"

"The head, you mean? I have no idea. I've seen it done before, on TV, but those things never look like real people to me. Still, we have little else, so it's worth a shot."

She nodded. "We'll see," she said, getting to her feet. "Come on, Lonnie. I was supposed to have been back in the office an hour ago. I'll talk to you later, Harry. Let me know how it goes with the head. In the meantime, we'll see you at De Luca's this afternoon."

Chapter 12

Samantha was a sweet kid, maybe twenty-three years old, tall, skinny, straight brown hair, glasses; she was the perfect match for Tim. I smiled to myself when he introduced her; it was obvious he was very fond of her.

"So, Samantha," I said. "What are your fees? How much is this thing going to cost me?"

"Please, Mr. Starke, call me Sam. If you'll pay for the materials and allow me to add it to my resume, that's all I need. I can get credit for it at school."

"Oh, the materials and credits are no problem, and I have a place for you to work here, but I can't allow you to work for noth... okay, okay, I get it. Tell you what: I'll buy you and Tim dinner. Good enough?"

She looked at Tim, eyebrows raised, and he nodded. She smiled at me, and the fee was agreed.

"How long will it take you to do the reconstruction," I asked, "and how close will it be to the original?"

"If I start this afternoon, and work full days, I might be able to get it finished by Friday evening. If I have a good skull to work with, that is. How like her will it be? I don't know. Close, I hope."

"Oh, the skull is a nice one.... Geeze, I'm sorry. That was inappropriate. We're talking about some poor girl, not an antique vase. You have a cast of the original, and it should be intact and clean, right, Tim?"

"Yes, it is. It should be easy to work with, not that I would know."

"Fine," I said. "Why don't you show her through to the empty office? Make sure she has everything she needs. If she needs anything, anything at all, you go get it for her. Okay?" It was, and they left. They could make a great couple.

Chapter 13

I parked the Explorer on the street outside the front of Il Sapore Roma, Salvatore De Luca's small but exclusive Italian restaurant. It's located on a dingy side street just off MLK. Back in the day, the 1930s, it had been a dry goods store. The old-fashioned interior was dark and narrow with room enough only for two single rows of six booths on either side of a central walkway that stretched from front to rear. At the far end, next to the kitchen and the restrooms, a small, semi-circular bar could seat up to six people, shoulder to shoulder, on tall stools.

Salvatore De Luca is the owner of record, but his connections to the mob run deep. Il Sapore Roma is a front for a whole range of illegal activities. Be that as it may, the food is authentic Italian, always good, and the restaurant is almost always busy, but not so much at two o'clock on a weekday afternoon.

I locked the car, undid the zipper on my coat, checked that the M&P9 was free in its holster, and pushed open the door to the restaurant. For a moment, I thought I was having a flashback, and I shuddered; not from fear, but from a weird feeling of *deja vu*. There they were; three of them, seated at the bar.

Sal had always reminded me of a vulture. Six feet three inches tall, thin as a rake; his face, long, narrow,

119

was accented by eyes almost hidden under hooded eyebrows. They were beady, black, and glittered in the artificial light. The great beak of a nose curved over a wide mouth, the corners of which were turned down at the corners in a grotesque caricature of an unhappy clown. When he smiled, which he rarely did, he exposed a set of perfect but badly stained teeth. He wore his lank, jet-black hair long, shoulder length, slicked back. As always, he was perched on a stool at the end of the bar close to the kitchen door, hunched over a drink, staring down into the depths of the glass.

As always, Sal was flanked by his two principle lieutenants. Both were big men. Tony Carpeta, whom I knew quite well, was wearing a nicely tailored suit, light gray. He was heavy-set, with receding black hair; his florid face was accented by a squashed nose and fat lips, and was set atop a double chin that oozed out over the collar of his black sweater. He looked like a slob, and he was; he was also fearless; at least he was when he had backup. On his own, not so much.

The second man, Jesus, I assumed, was almost as big, dark skin, bushy black hair, Zapata mustache. He was obviously Hispanic, and less well dressed than Carpeta: jeans, thick leather belt with an oval silver buckle inlaid with gold, a white shirt, and a black leather vest, Mexican style. *How appropriate.*

I've met his kind before: the stereotypical minor drug lord from south of the border. This one's a killer, if ever I saw one.

"Hey, Sal," I said, as I strolled the walkway between the twin rows of booths. "I hear you're looking for me."

"Well, well." He twisted his head sideways to look upward at me, you know, like a chicken does. "If it ain't Sherlock friggin' Starke. You gotta a goddamn nerve walkin' in here; must have a death wish. Oh yes, I *do* want to see you, Starke. I wanna see you bad. I wanna see you pay for what you did to me an' Gino. I wanna see you dead."

He held up his right hand. The little finger was missing above the first joint. "You piece of shit. You smashed it so bad they couldn't put it together again; you'll pay for that. Gino? He was family, a cousin, you'll pay for that, too."

"Sal. You and Gino both got exactly what you deserved. In fact, you got away with murder. If Gino hadn't died that day, you would right now be facing life for solicitation to murder. You and I both know what he did to James Westwood was on your orders. We had him dead to rights. You should be thanking me. Damn, Sal, you even got your twelve mil back."

"Screw you, Starke. You had nothin', an' you killed Gino, an' you're gonna pay."

121

"Sal, I assume that all of this is because I went to see Billy Dickerson yesterday? What's your connection to him? He supplying you with girls?"

"What the hell are you talking about, Starke? Who the hell is Billy Dickerson?"

"Oh, for Christ's sake, Sal. Don't go there. I know you and Dickerson are joined at the hip. At least, he's joined to your hip. What's that about?"

"Again, and I'll say it just once more, I don't know any Billy Dickerson. Now get the hell out of here." *Oh hell yes, you know him. You know him very well.*

"In a minute. I'm not finished yet—"

"You're goddamn finished when I say you're finished. Now go... Tony."

Tony twitched nervously; I didn't blame him.

"Sal. I'm investigating the murder of a teenage girl. Dickerson's a procurer; you're into prostitution, big time; you're in bed together. I will find out what happened to her, you can bet on it. If I find out that you and Dickerson had anything to do with it, I'll take you down, Sal. I'll take you down hard."

The room was quiet. I could almost hear De Luca thinking. His boys were silent. Tony Carpeta was twisting a napkin nervously between his fingers. Jesus had one elbow on the bar and a nasty grin on his face.

"Let me tell you something, Starke," De Luca said, after what seemed an eternity. "You screwed me over once. It won't happen again. I had nothing to do with any dead homeless kid. You got that? One more thing, Starke. I'm gonna see you dead, and when I say see you, I'm gonna look down on your body and piss on it."

It was no idle threat; I could tell by his body language and the tone of his voice. I also knew that he wouldn't make such a threat in front of his subordinates if he didn't intend to carry it out. That would mean a loss of face, not something De Luca would allow. He was coming after me.

"I'm very patient," he said, quietly. "I can wait, an' enjoy knowing you'll be looking over your shoulder, looking into the shadows, wondering, if and when... an' one day, Starke, it will happen. Until then, we'll be watching you. It could be a day, it could be a couple of years. Have a nice life, Harry Starke." He smiled that toothy, barracuda-like grimace I remembered so well. "Enjoy what time you have left. I know I will." The look on his face was pure evil. "Oh, and do tell your friends to be careful, too. It's a dangerous world out there."

"I hope that's not a threat, Sal. I can handle your bullshit, and I can handle your two mutts. So let me say this, and you know me well enough to know that I mean every word of it. If either one of these two

123

idiots come anywhere near me or mine, I'll have 'em fitted for a wooden overcoat, and then I'll come after you. I'll put you in wheelchair for the rest of your days. Not only that, the only way you'll be able to eat will be through a straw, because I'll take every last one of those filthy tombstones you call teeth, and I'll bust all seven remaining fingers and both thumbs. You got that?"

He wasn't the least bit perturbed. In fact, I truly think he found it all a big joke.

"Get outa here, Starke. You're pathetic. Show him the door, Tony." He turned away, placed his elbows on the bar, and hunched over his drink.

Tony was not quite so dismissive, nor was he enthusiastic about showing me out. I'm sure he remembered only too well what had happened to him the last time he'd tried it with me. More to the point, he was there when I pumped two hollow points into his one-time partner, Gino Polti. Anyway, he looked at Sal, got no reaction, and I could see by the look on his face that he didn't know what to do. His new partner, however, was a different story. He started to rise from his stool.

"Sit down, Pancho," I said. "I don't want to have to hurt you. By the way, you need a haircut. You look like a neglected poodle." He glared at me, his eyes narrowed, his mouth twisted in a snarl. I slid my right hand under my coat and felt for the grip of the M&P9.

"Take it easy, both of you," I said. "I know my way out."

Jesus lowered himself back onto the stool.

"Just a word of advice, Jesus. Talk to your friend, Tony, here. Ask him what happens to turds like you that think they're better than me. Ask him about Gino."

I turned my back on all three of them and walked confidently toward the door. Confident was not exactly how I felt, though. The back of my neck itched. I could feel their eyes boring into me as I walked. Yeah, it was bravado, all for show, and about as stupid a sham as I'd ever pulled. The fact that I got away with it is no kudos to me. I just got lucky, that's all.

When the door closed behind me, I took a deep breath, and shook my head, appalled at my own stupidity. Then I grinned, unlocked the car door, and got inside. *Damned fool. Why the hell didn't you just hand De Luca your damn firearm?*

Yeah, I'd gotten away with it, but for how long? De Luca wasn't one to make idle promises. I'd need to keep my wits about me, and so would those near and dear to me. That bothered me a whole lot, just as Sal had intended it should.

For myself, I wasn't that worried. Kate? I wasn't worried about her either. She was more than able to look after herself. Amanda? Not so much. I'd need to talk to them both, but Amanda I'd need to teach a few of the basics. My staff? Bob, Heather, Jacque, Mike, I could handle them. Our two secretaries, Leslie and Margo, they were going to cost me. *Oh hell. I need to get everybody together.*

I looked around, up and down the street. *Where the hell are Kate and Lonnie? Oh, I see.*

They were parked about a hundred yards away, at the far end of the street, in a lot where once a building, now demolished, had stood. I looked at my watch. It was a little after three-thirty. I hit the Bluetooth and called Kate. Then I called the office.

"Jacque," I said when she answered the phone. "How many of the staff are in the office right now? All but Heather. Okay. Don't let anyone leave. Get them all together in the conference room. I need to talk to them. I'll be there in... oh, less than ten minutes."

I hit the starter button.... *Oh shit....* I closed my eyes and held my breath. Nothing. I heaved a sigh, shook my head, and swung the Explorer out into the traffic. *You gotta think, Harry boy. Next time there's likely to be an unpleasant surprise.*

I parked the car in the office lot, took a deep breath, opened the door, and very carefully eased myself out of the car. *Whew. Nothing. Geeze, Harry. You're damned paranoid. Yeah, better that than spread all over the lot. This needs thinking about.*

I locked the car and looked around; Lonnie's cruiser pulled in through the gate and he parked beside the Explorer. I waited for them, and then headed for the office door. I breezed in, headed straight for the Keurig and punched up a cup of Dark Italian Roast, then the three of us headed for the conference room, followed by a worried-looking Jacque Hale.

"Okay, everyone," I said, as I sat down at the head of the table and looked around. "We have a problem. Kate, Lonnie, I asked you here because I wanted you to be aware of what's going on.

"As I said, we have a problem; at least I do, but I'm sorry to have to tell you, it affects all of us. I've just been to see Sal De Luca. It was not a pleasant meeting. He's planning on revenge for the damage I did back in August. He made threats against me, and by proxy, that means he made threats against all of you, too."

"What kind of threats?" Bob asked.

"He said he's going to make me pay for what I did to his hand and for killing Gino. Seems he was a cousin. He didn't say how or when, which was part of his strategy: a form of terrorism. It worked, too. I had a couple of nasty moments out there."

"So how does that affect us?" Ronnie asked.

"I'm not sure that it does, but he could decide to get at me through one of you. Whatever, I'd rather be safe than sorry."

"So what's the plan?" Bob asked.

"First off, we'll need to take precautions, all of us. Then we need to handle the problem, which is De Luca."

Bob nodded, his face set, serious.

I continued, "As I've said many times, the parking lot gates are to be kept closed and locked at all times. Yeah, I know. I'm the worst offender, but not anymore. It's a pain in the ass, but it has to be done. Jacque, make a note; see what it would take to have an automatic gate installed out there." *Why the hell haven't I thought of that before?*

"Second," I continued. "From now on, everyone, except for Mike and the girls, carries a firearm at all times; you, too, Jacque. Mike, you go for weapons training starting tonight. Kate, can you fast-track him through the carry permit procedure?"

She nodded.

"Bob, I'm sorry, buddy, but you're gonna have to babysit Leslie and Margo to and from work. When you can't do it, I'll do it."

"Are you sure all this is necessary?" Jacque asked.

"Nope. Not really, but I'd rather do it than be sorry later. Now, before I move on, any questions?" There were none.

"Now, I said the gates to the lot must be kept closed and locked at all time, and I meant it. If any one of you violates that rule, until further notice, I will suspend you without pay. Got it?" They all nodded.

"I hate to frighten y'all, and if anyone wants to quit their job, I'll totally understand; your jobs will be waiting for you when this is all over. You *need* to be frightened. De Luca is a psychopath; he has no conscience and won't hesitate to kill or maim if he thinks it will hurt me. Now, does anyone want to quit? No. So be it. Bob and I will do our best to protect you."

I reached for my coffee, sipped on it, thinking, wondering if what I was about to do next was over the line. *Screw it. They need to know what we're up against.*

I looked at each one of them in turn, then said, "Most of you already know this, but for those who don't, I'll go over it. Car bombs come in several types, any one of which Sal De Luca is quite capable of using. There's the basic type that goes off at the turn of the ignition switch or press of the starter button. The second is a pressure-operated switch usually located under the driver's seat; it could be triggered when you sit down or when you get up off the seat. The third is, of course, triggered remotely, either by a wireless switch or a cell phone."

I looked at their faces. Mike's was white, so was Leslie's.

"Look. I'm probably making more of this than I should," I said, "but we do need to take care. Make sure you put your cars away at night; lock your garage doors. Don't leave them *anywhere* unattended. If you do have to leave them, try always to have someone with you; have them stay in the car until you return. Jacque, call Tom Skerrett and have him set up surveillance cameras in the parking lot, and to cover the streets both ways, front and rear. I want them installed today. If he can't do it today, find someone who will, and I want an answer on the feasibility of an automatic gate *today*." Inwardly, I shook my head. I didn't want the crew to have any idea how really worried I was. *Yep, you really are paranoid, Harry.... Am I taking this too far, I wonder? Nope. Don't think so.*

"Okay. That's it for now. Bob, Kate. My office, please." I got up from my seat and walked though

130

into my refuge. Bob followed me, still limping slightly, with the aid of a stick.

"What the hell have you gotten yourself into, Harry?" he asked as he lowered himself into one of the leather easy chairs.

"It was something I went looking for," I said, dropping into the seat beside his. "I had a call from Benny Hinkle; a warning. Couldn't believe it. Benny isn't, after all, my best friend."

"Oh, it was a back-handed gift," he said. "He's paying De Luca protection. Maybe he thinks you can get him off his back."

"Now that's something I didn't know, but why would I? Where did you get it from?"

"It's general knowledge. Benny does a lot of business. You know De Luca. He wants his cut. So, Harry. Tell me what the hell is going on. What are we up against?"

I really appreciated that he had said, 'we'.

Kate looked first at Bob, then at me, but she didn't say a word. She didn't need to. The expression on her face said it all. She was angry, very angry.

I told them about my visit to Sal and about the threats he'd made. They listened carefully to every word. When I'd finished, Bob leaned his head back in the chair, steepled his fingers, and stared up at the ceiling.

"We've got to put a stop to it," he said. "We can't operate like this, not for long, anyway, looking over our shoulders."

"That's what he wants," I said. "It may all be bullshit. He may have no intention of doing any one of us violence, just to put the fear of God into me, but.... Well, it's working. That son of a bitch is capable of anything."

"So. Do you have a plan?" Kate asked.

"Short of killin' his ass? Nope. What about you, Bob? Any ideas?"

"Killin' his ass sounds good to me. Just gotta do it right. Leave it to me." He started to get up out of his seat.

"Oh, Jesus Christ," Kate said. "I didn't need to hear that. Goddamnit, Bob."

"Hey, whoa; she's right." I all but shouted it at him. "What the hell do think you're doing? You can't just go kill him."

"Now did I say I was going to do that? No! Of course I didn't. Thing is though...."

"NO! Absolutely not. I mean it, Bob. We'll both end up in Brushy Mountain for the rest of our days. We'll let it play out for a while; see what, if anything, he has in mind. Right?"

He was standing now, leaning on his cane, looking down at me, smiling, and I didn't like it. I'd seen that smile before, and it boded no one any good.

"I mean it, Bob. We'll do nothing, for now; play it by ear; see what happens."

He nodded, reluctantly, I could tell, and then, still smiling, he turned and walked out of the office, closing the door behind him. *Oh my God. He'll do it.*

"Shit, Harry," Kate said. "You've stirred up one hell of a hornet's nest. Bob's even crazier than you are, which is saying something, but if he kills De Luca.... I'll do what I can, but I won't be able to protect you."

"Kate, you know me, better than most. Over the years I've been accused of all sorts of misdeeds, and of skirting the law by a lot of people, including the DA, the chief of police, the sheriff, and even the FBI. I've been hauled in for interrogation... once by you, and I've even been locked up, but none of it ever stuck. I can handle this. De Luca has called the play. I have to protect my people; I'll do whatever it takes. I won't let Bob loose, not if I can help it."

"That's the point, though, isn't it? He's just like you. He'll do what it takes to protect you, whatever it is. You won't be able to stop him."

"Kate, you've known me a long time. You have to have faith. You have to trust me."

She just shook her head, got up out of her seat, looked down at me, turned, and without a word or a backward glance, walked out of the door. I leaned back in my chair, put my hands behind my head, and closed my eyes. *Oh my God. This is not good.*

I looked at my watch. It was after three o'clock. *She'll be at the station, preparing for tonight's broadcast. I wonder....*

I grabbed my iPhone and punched the speed dial. She answered on the second ring.

"Hello, Harry," Amanda said. "Is it important? I'm editing."

"Yep, it is. I need to see you. See if you can get someone to cover the eleven o'clock broadcast for you. I'll pick you up at the station after the six o'clock broadcast. Okay?"

"Well... yes, but... what is it? What's wrong?"

"It's nothing to worry about, not right now, at least. Just trust me, okay?"

She hesitated, then agreed. I said goodbye and disconnected.

Chapter 14

I was waiting for her when she exited Channel 7's front door. As always, she looked stunning: same white parka, gloves, wooly hat, boots; this time she had on black furry earmuffs and was clutching a leather handbag big enough to house my Explorer. She looked like she'd stepped right off the front cover of *Vogue Magazine.*

"Hey. Over here," I shouted out of the car window.

She turned, cocked her head to one side, spotted me, smiled, and hurried over. "Whoa, nice ride, Jimbob. That all they had?"

"Hey. It's discreet, right? Hop in. We've got stuff to do."

"What about my car?" she said, looking round at her Lexus.

"You can leave it here. I'll bring you to work in the morning. Okay?"

"Smooth, Harry. Very smooth. Okay, but I need to let the front desk know. Back in a jiffy." She hurried away, still clutching the big bag to her. She was back in less than a minute and climbed up into the Explorer beside me.

"So, what the hell is so urgent?"

"You'll see. We're going to have some fun. Then a nice meal, and then I'm going to take you home with me and treat you like a princess."

"Hmmm," she said, looking at me sideways. "Nice meal sounds good; not sure about the princess thing; slut might be better."

I grinned at her. "That, I can manage." Then I punched the starter and pulled out of the lot.

Fifteen minutes later, I pulled into the lot in front of Shooter's Depot on Shallowford Road. They carry a wide selection of firearms and they have an indoor firing range. I've been doing business there for years.

"Harry...."

"It's okay, just bear with me okay?" I parked right in front of the entrance, where the car could be seen by the staff inside.

"Come on," I said. I waited until she climbed down and joined me, then I locked the door, took her arm, and escorted her into the store; she was still clutching that damn great bag.

"Harry, please tell me what's going on."

"I told you. We're going to have some fun, and then... well, we'll see. Take off your gloves."

She pursed her lips, rolled her eyes, and did as she was asked.

"I'd like to see a Glock 26 and a Sig P239, please," I told the clerk. The two handguns were duly placed upon the counter and the cases opened. I took the Glock, inserted the mag, and handed it to her.

"How does that feel? Comfortable?"

She held it away from her, as if it would bite.

"Here, like this." I took it from her, grabbed her right hand, fitted the weapon into the palm of her hand, and wrapped her fingers around the grip. "Now how does it feel?"

"I hate it. Why are you doing this?"

I didn't answer. I took the Glock from her and handed her the Sig. "Try that one."

"I hate it, too."

I took it from her, turned to the clerk, handed it to him, and said, "We'll take the Glock. Gimme some shells and a loader and start the paperwork. It's for her."

"No, Harry," she said. "I hate guns."

"I know you do, sweetheart, but this is important. Please trust me. I'll explain later."

Reluctantly, she nodded her head and filled out the paperwork. Five minutes later, she was approved, and we headed for the range.

The nine millimeter Glock 26, some call it the Baby Glock, came with two mags. I loaded both of

137

them, put them both on the shelf next to the weapon, handed her a set of ear protectors and safely glasses, put my own over my ears, sent the target to the five-yard position, and pulled my own M&P9. I looked sideways at her. She looked terrified. I grinned at her, worked the slide on my nine, and emptied the mag into the target.

"Not too bad. Six-inch group, a little loose, but not bad," I said, as I hit the switch and brought the target home, and then looked at her. I almost laughed out loud. She had her hands clamped over the cups of the protectors and her eyes screwed tight shut.

"Hey," I said, loudly, and tapped her on the shoulder. She kept her hands on the protectors, twisted her head sideways, opened one eye, and squinted up at me.

"Finished? You ass," she yelled, taking off the glasses and protectors.

"Your turn," I said, loading a clip into the Glock and working the action.

"Not on your life, Harry Starke."

I could see she meant it, so I sighed, removed my glasses, and pulled her to a seat along the back wall.

"Okay," I said. "I'll explain. I have a problem, a very big problem, which means everyone close to me also has a problem."

"Oh my God. What have you done?"

"Me? Nothing. I did, however, have a rather nasty encounter with our friend, Sal De Luca. He swears he's going to make me pay for killing Gino, and for the loss of his pinky finger. I believe him. It means that anyone connected with me is in danger. I have everyone, well almost everyone, who works for me carrying a firearm. I want you to carry one, too. Kate will expedite the carry permit."

She stared at me, eyes wide, face pale. She was frightened and, at that moment, the most beautiful thing I had ever seen.

"It's okay. We'll—"

"It's not okay, you friggin' idiot. You can't protect me all the time and I'm scared to death of guns." There were tears rolling down her cheeks. I felt like a total shit.

"I know. That's why we're here. Look, I'm a licensed instructor; we can do this; we can qualify you. It takes eight hours; we can do that over the next few days. This Glock is a lovely little weapon. Kate carries one. Come on. Give it a try." And, bless her, so she did. She did better than give it a try.

An hour later, she was handling the Glock like she'd been doing it all her life. She still was a bit wild with her aim. Even so, by the time we left the range, she could hit the silhouette of a man at five yards ten times out of ten, and she could load and work the weapon like a pro. I was damned proud of her, and although she wouldn't admit it, I could tell she was proud of herself. I didn't tell her that hitting a target was one thing, hitting a real live person was something else again. *She done good. No point in squelching her confidence.*

We put the Glock into her bag, where she could get at it, and we got out of there. Fifteen minutes later, at just after eight o'clock, we were shoveling Chinese food in our mouths. She was, by the look of it, even hungrier than I was.

By nine-thirty, we were outside my home on Lakeshore Lane. I was about to pull into the garage when I suddenly had a wierd feeling,. I looked down the road, past my condo. Unfortunately, there were no streetlights, but the night was clear and there was enough light from the neighboring buildings for me to see that there was a car parked at the roadside some hundred yards away. Normally, I would have driven on past, just to be nosy, but I had Amanda with me, and if it turned out to be.... Well, I didn't want to put her in danger.

I hit the garage door opener, drove inside, closed the door, went up the stairs to the kitchen and set the security alarm. She reached for the light switch, but I stopped her.

"Hold on. I need to take a quick look out the window."

She looked at me, bemused.

"It's okay," I said. "Probably nothing." I cracked the blind with a finger and peered through. The car was gone. I didn't feel comfortable. I turned on the lights, went to the refrigerator, grabbed a bottle of Pinot Grigio and two glasses, and then we both settled onto the couch in front of the picture window. I grabbed the remote and dimmed the lights. As the lights went down, so the great river came to life in front of us. A light breeze was whipping the surface of the water, and it sparkled and shimmered from the lights of the Thrasher Bridge.

I spent the next thirty minutes filling her in on what had transpired during my visit to Sal De Luca and the precautions I'd implemented. She listened without interrupting until I had finished, then she stood up and, wine glass in hand, walked to the window and stood looking out over the water. It was a rare sight, and one I was well content to enjoy.

She stood with her back to me, legs slightly apart, glass in her right hand, her left hand closed to a fist rested on her hip. Her hips and head were cocked slightly to the right, most of her weight was on her right leg. Her skirt tight against her legs was cut four inches above the knee, and thus she was silhouetted against the lights across the river: stunning.

She must have stood like that, thinking, for five minutes, maybe more, and then she turned and looked down at me. "Harry, what the hell are we going to do?"

I could see she was very worried. I thought for a moment, a glib answer on the tip of my tongue, but I thought better of it. I decided to be brutally honest with her.

"Amanda, I have no idea. De Luca is a psychopath, a killer. I don't think it will end until one of us is dead, and I don't plan on that being me."

She looked at me, horrified, raised her glass, emptied it in one huge mouthful, and poured herself another. Then she came over and sat down beside me.

"Damn it, Harry. I don't want to lose you." There were tears in her eyes. I shook my head. At that moment, I think I was more pissed off than I have ever been.

"You're not going to. I promise." *Now that was a damn fool thing to say.*

"Look, I don't know how this is going to play out. The only thing I can do is wait for De Luca to make his move; then end it, quickly. If I have to kill him, I will."

She didn't answer. She just cuddled up against me and sipped on her wine. It was nice, but it wasn't, if you get my meaning. I was as tight as a goddamn drum and my head was splitting. I needed a shower, and I needed some sleep.

"Come on," I said, standing up and taking her by the hand. "Let's get some sleep. I need to get you out of here early in the morning. I know you have clothes in the spare room. Do you have anything you can wear tomorrow?"

She stood, nodded, and said, "I have jeans and a turtleneck. They'll do."

"Maybe you should...."

"What?"

"I dunno. I was just thinking. Would you like to stay here, just until this thing with De Luca is over? I don't mind taking you to and from work. I'd feel better if I could keep an eye on you."

"Oh my God. You are such a sweetie... but...."

"No buts," I said. "It's just temporary, a precaution."

"But what about Kate?"

"What about her? It's over. Has been for months. It's none of her business."

"So you say. Do you not see the way she looks at you?"

"Geeze, Amanda. The woman barely talks to me. Look. It's done. I'll take you to work in the morning, pick you up from the station around ten-thirty, then we'll go to your place, you can pack some clothes, and then we'll go shopping and come back to Castle Lakeshore Lane. What do you say?"

"What the hell..." she said, "yes."

Chapter 15

The following morning, I dropped Amanda off at Channel 7 and went to my office. I grinned when I saw the gate to the lot closed and locked. *Hah, that's a first. My little talk must have hit home.*

When I got out of the car to unlock the gate, I suddenly felt vulnerable, so much so the back of my neck itched. I looked around; nothing. I parked the car, closed the gate, and went into the outer office through the side door. Jacque was at her desk.

"Good morning, Jacque," I said, as I headed for the Keurig. "Any word on an automatic gate?"

"Yes, I talked to Overhead Doors late yesterday afternoon. They were out here this morning. They can get one installed today... but it's going to be—"

"Yeah, I know. Expensive. I don't care. Get it done. I want it in and working before we leave tonight. I had a bad feeling just now when I was unlocking the gate. We don't need to be getting out of our vehicles."

"I knew you'd say that. I placed the order with the foreman before he left. They'll be here by nine this morning and they won't leave until it's finished."

I grinned at her. *That's my girl.*

"What about Skerrett? Can he do the cameras?"

"He can. He's already on his way. I'll let you know when he gets here."

Now I was feeling better. I took my coffee, went into the office, and flopped down into my throne behind the desk. I had one more chore to do before I could get on with my day; it was one I was dreading. I took a deep breath, hit the speed dial on my iPhone, and called Kate. *This should just about finish things between us.*

"Good morning, Harry. What do you need?"

I filled her in on the precautions I was taking, that I thought someone had been watching my home, and then I told her about my fitting Amanda with a firearm. She agreed that it was a good idea and said she would indeed expedite the concealed carry process for her.

"Anything else, Harry?"

I closed my eyes. "Look, Kate, I know how this is going to sound, but it's not what you think. Amanda is going to stay with me until this thing with De Luca is over."

"Good idea, Harry. The lady is a bit of a ditz. She'd make a good target. When are you moving her in?" *Damn. That was easy.*

I didn't know what to say. I just sat there, thinking.

"Harry? You still there?"

146

"Er... yes. Kate...."

"Oh stop it," she interrupted. "What did you think I would say? Amanda is a wonderful person, a bit flakey at times, but I like her, a lot. De Luca is a head case. She's an obvious target. You did good. Now, do you need anything else?"

"No, not now. Thanks, Kate. I'll call you later, when I know where the hell I am at."

I looked at my watch. It was just after nine-thirty; I'd promised to pick Amanda up at ten-thirty. I had time to do a little thinking. I grabbed another cup of coffee and settled down. I put De Luca out of my mind. *Oh yeah, sure you did.*

Jacque poked her head in the door. "Tom Skerrett is here."

"Show him in." She did.

"Hey, Tom. What do you have for me?"

"I have cameras, a recorder, and I'll hook everything up so y'all can monitor it on your iPhones."

"Hi-def cameras, right? I don't want that cheap black and white crap. I want to be able to identify people, intruders."

He nodded. "I anticipated that. This system has eight cameras, four for the exterior and four for inside. The recorder has a three-terabyte hard drive good for thirty days of recording, more if you use the system in motion detection mode. It has good night vision and, as I said, you can monitor the system on your iPhone. It's a good outfit. I wouldn't offer you anything less."

"You can install it today?" He nodded. "Good. Let's do it." We shook hands and he left.

I took a fresh legal pad and a mechanical pencil from the desk door, flipped open the pad, and stared at it; the blank page stared back at me. I wrote the date and time, threw the pencil down on the desk, leaned back in the chair, hoisted my feet up onto the desk, folded my arms and closed my eyes.

The next thing I knew, my cell phone was buzzing, walking across the top of the desk. I grabbed it and looked at the screen. Amanda.

"Where the hell are you?" she asked; she was agitated.

I looked at my watch. It was 10:45. I'd slept for almost an hour.

"Geeze, Amanda. I'm sorry. I got tied up. I'm leaving now. Stay inside and wait for me."

I grabbed my heavy coat, checked the shoulder rig and the M&P9, and rushed out the door.

"Damn, Jacque," I said, as I passed her desk. "Why the hell did you let me sleep like that?"

"I...."

"Never mind," I said. "No harm done. Back after lunch. Hold the fort." *No harm done, my ass.*

Out in the lot, they were already at work. The old gate was down and Tom Skerrett was on the roof installing a camera on the corner of the building. Fifteen minutes later, I walked into Channel 7's reception area. Amanda wasn't there.

"She's in her office," the girl behind the desk said. "I'll let her know you're here, Mr. Starke."

"Not a good start, Harry," she said and she stalked past me and out of the building.

"Hey," I said, grabbing her arm as she reached for the handle of the car door. "I'm sorry. Hell, Amanda. I fell asleep at my desk."

"You what? You fell asleep?" She glared at me, then her face softened, she smiled, and then she started laughing.

"What?"

"You, falling asleep. I never was much, Harry. Now I know how you really feel about me." She was joking, I could tell, I hoped.

When we arrived at her apartment building, I drove around the block, looking for anything out of the ordinary; nothing, but it was right then when I realized just how well De Luca's strategy was working. In the space of less than forty-eight hours, my world, and that of those around me, had been turned upside down. *But not for long, damn it; not if I can help it.*

I'd been in Amanda's apartment only once before. She wasn't one to live high off the hog. It was comfortable, efficient, a place to sleep, and that was about all. But she did have a lot of clothes.

"Oh my God, Amanda," I said, as she started to fill a fourth suitcase. "That's enough. Hell, I didn't ask you to come live with me, just to stay for a few days."

"I know. These should last five, maybe six days. I do need several changes, you know, for work. Besides, you might like having me around."

"Damn," I muttered. "No wonder I like living alone."

"What's that?"

"Nothing... nothing. Look, you can have my spare bedroom. The closet should be big enough." *Hell, maybe it won't.*

"Not on your life, Big Boy. You think I'm gonna live with you and sleep in the spare room. Think again. I'm gonna wear you out, Buddy."

I grinned and shook my head. *Might not be so bad after all.*

I dropped her off at my place so she could unpack. I didn't need to take her to work; she'd arranged to take some vacation time. I told her to

150

stay put, not to open the door to anyone but me, and then I headed back to the office. It was lunchtime.

Chapter 16

When I got back to the office, the new gate was already in place; it just wasn't working yet. Be that as it may, I didn't want to leave my car on the street, so I had the workers move it out of the way and let me through. They did, with much mumbling and complaining. It took four of them to move the heavy gate.

Inside, Tom Skerrett was showing Jacque and Bob how the camera system worked. He looked at me with his eyebrows raised. I waved my hand for him to continue; Jacque could show me how it all worked later.

I went to my office and called Kate.

"Hey," I said, when she answered. "You want to get some lunch?"

"Sure. When?"

"I'm thinking Steak & Shake on Gunbarrel. That work for you?"

She said it would, and that she'd meet me there in thirty minutes. I parked the car in front of the window where I knew I would be able to see it from inside the restaurant. I was waiting for her when she arrived. As always, she looked great, and I suffered a moment of regret. *All those years....*

"So what did you want, Harry?" she said, as we waited for the receptionist to seat us. It was busy; always is.

"Oh a couple of things.... I miss our times together, Kate."

"Me, too, but it was your choice, Harry. Now we both have to live with it. Why are you bringing this up now? Is it Amanda?"

"No, and I don't know. I need to talk to you about Hill House."

"Well, I was about to call you. CSI found another body. In the basement, well, in the old drainage system. There's an iron grill down there. Doc Sheddon's not sure yet, but he thinks it's been down there a long time. Could be connected. We'll see."

I can't say I was surprised. Where there's one body, there's often more, sometimes several more.

"Male?" I asked. "Female?"

"We don't know yet. What's left of it is a mess... you don't want to know. How's the head?"

"It's fine. Why do you ask?"

"Not *your* head, dummy. The reconstruction?"

"Oh that. Coming along. She started yesterday and is working full time. I hope it will be finished tomorrow."

153

The waiter arrived, and we ordered. I had a mushroom steakburger; Kate had chicken taco salad

"Listen, Kate. I'm really bothered about this mess with De Luca. You're looking out for yourself, right?"

She rolled her eyes.

"Okay, I get it. Now. I have a real bad feeling about the Dickersons. I think they are hand in glove with De Luca. How, I don't know yet, but I'll find out. The Draycotts? I think something stinks there, too, though what it might be I have no idea. Both of them talk a good game, but something just doesn't jell with me. Not sure what Bob thinks, but I'm going to sit down with him when I get back to the office. One thing I do know is that Bob doesn't like Sam Draycott, and I trust his instincts."

"What do you mean, something doesn't jell?"

"I don't know. I'm reasonably certain that what they're doing is on the up and up, but there was something I just couldn't put my finger on: the tone of his voice, sometimes; body language; whatever. It'll come to me, but.... Look, I know damn well they know, or knew, the Dickersons. Why would they hide that?"

She shook her head, content just to sit and listen to me ramble on. The truth was that I didn't have a good feel for either organization.

I sat there, stirring my coffee, daydreaming; I was away with the birds. Odd, hazy, disconnected thoughts ran through my head.

"Hey. You still with me?"

"Oh, sorry," I said. "Look, I need to get back. Call you later?"

"Of course. Anytime. By the way. Did you get Amanda moved in?"

"Yeah, I did." I didn't elaborate. I didn't want to, and I sure didn't want to sit looking at the smirk.

"I'll call you when I figure it out. Oh, and let me know what Doc Sheddon comes up with on the body in the drain. Later?"

"Yeah, later."

I left her there, staring after me. I could see her watching through the window as I got into the car.

Back at the office, I visited Samantha in the back office. She was hard at work. The head looked weird, all dark brown muscle with little white studs sticking out of it.

"How's it going, Sam? Have you had lunch? You need anything?"

She turned and looked at me, smiling. "Do you always converse in questions, Mr. Starke? Fine, yes, and no."

I grinned at her. "Think you'll finish it tomorrow?"

"I was hoping so, but...."

"Well, don't stress over it. I need it to be a good job, a real likeness. Take your time. She's been dead a long time. A couple of days will make no difference to her now. Just make sure you get it right."

She smiled at me, obviously relieved. "I will. I promise."

"Okay, Samantha. I don't want you here over the weekend. Do what you can, then start over on Monday morning."

She agreed.

I went to my office. I beckoned for Bob to join me. "Hey. How's the ankle?"

"Better," he said, leaning his cane against my desk.

"You thought anymore about our interviews with the Dickersons and Draycotts?"

"I've thought about little else. Dickerson is pimping, for sure. Draycott... I don't like him, or her, but I think they're probably legit."

He thought for a moment then continued, "This thing with De Luca. We have to fix it. He's already turned this place into a circus, and he's not going to

156

quit. That means we're either gonna have to take him out, or send him down. Your choice."

I didn't like what he was saying, but I knew he was right.

"What have you got in mind?" I asked, not really wanting to hear the answer.

"I've been talking to Tim. Look, if he's in cahoots with Dickerson, we should be able to put them both away. Tim thinks we should look at them both for trafficking. If we can get them for that, they will go away for a long time."

"You think? Bob, this is Chattanooga, not Chicago." Bob is from Chi Town.

"Yeah, that's what I said to him."

I picked up the phone and punched the button for Tim's extension.

"What's this about trafficking?" I asked when he came in.

"It happens, and you have two shady characters in Dickerson and De Luca. If they are forcing girls to... well, you know. That's the classic definition. It's not something I know a whole lot about, but...."

I nodded, picked up my cell phone and punched the speed dial for Kate.

"Harry. What can I do for you?"

"I need some information. What do you know about human trafficking?"

"I know it's a big problem, bigger than you can imagine, but I'm Homicide. That's a whole 'nother department, and it's not something I'm that familiar with. Why do you want to know?"

"Not sure yet, but it might be something. Look, I need to know how prevalent human trafficking is here in Chattanooga, how big of a problem it is. Can you help?"

"Maybe. Let me contact some people, see what I can find out. I'll call you back when I have something. Talk to you later." Click! *Damn it. I wish she wouldn't do that. I wanted to ask her.... Ah, screw it.*

Chapter 17

Kate called back at a little after three o'clock that afternoon. Said she had someone she wanted me to meet. I told her to come on over. She arrived some thirty minutes later accompanied by a woman I judged to be in her early thirties. Jacque showed the two of them into the conference room where I was talking to Bob.

"Harry," Kate said. "This is Sergeant Sarah Lennon. You asked what I knew, about trafficking. Well, as I said, I know very little about it, so I checked with our Special Victims Unit. Sarah has agreed to share what she can. Is now a good time?"

I looked at Bob. He shrugged. "Better get Heather in here, and maybe Tim."

I nodded, shoved my head out of the door, and called for them to join us. They did.

"Thanks for your time, Sergeant," I said, holding out my hand.

She took it; her grip was firm, strong even. "Please, call me Sarah."

"Sarah, then. Please, take a seat. This is my lead investigator, Bob Ryan, and this is Heather Stillwell, and Tim Clarke is my expert in all things to do with computers. So what can you tell us?"

"Before I try to do that, why don't you tell me why you're interested? That way, I can tailor the information to your needs."

"Did Kate not tell you about the body they found under the floor of Hill House?"

"She did, but she didn't tell me how trafficking is related to a homicide, and a cold one at that."

I nodded. "The house, during the period we're interested in, was used as a homeless shelter. Two separate entities were involved; both of them were in the same business. They still are today, but at different locations. We think at least one of them is involved in pimping, perhaps worse."

"Would I know these people?" she asked.

I looked at Kate, who nodded.

"William Dickerson is running what he calls—"

"I know him," Sarah interrupted. "He's running some sort of weird home on Cherry. Who's the other?"

"The Draycotts."

"I know them, too. As far as we know, they are legitimate. The Dickersons though; we've had our eye on them for quite a while, but so far we've found nothing to hang him with. If they're into anything illegal, they're keeping it well under wraps."

"What about Salvatore De Luca?" I asked.

"Yes. We know him quite well. Very professional. Very slick. Very dirty. He's mobbed up. He also has a team of lawyers at his disposal. We haven't been able to touch him either."

"Well," I said, "we're looking at all three of them, though I think you may be right about the Draycotts. Dickerson... well, I know he's running girls. No," I said, as she was about to speak. "I don't have any proof; it's just a gut feeling based on observation. So?" I looked at her, questioningly.

"The answer to your question is that human trafficking in this area is prevalent. The general public has no idea what's going on here and in the county and its surrounds, and it's getting worse, but it's not all what you think it is."

"How do you mean?" I asked.

"More than fifty percent of all prostitution in the state involving minors is family oriented: usually the pimps are the girls' fathers."

I looked at her, aghast. So did Tim.

"You're kidding," I said.

"Nope. We have a rather unique problem in this area; most of the Southern states do. Sex between family members has been widely accepted as the norm here for generations. That being so, it's easy to understand that a man who needs to make a payment on his truck will consider his daughter a readymade

161

source of income; he simply sells her to anyone willing to pay. That's trafficking, of a sort. After the first time, when they find out how easy it is, they do it repeatedly. Eventually, it becomes the norm."

We all stared at her.

"I had no idea," I said.

"Very few people do, but it's bad. The Tennessee Bureau of Investigation issued a report for August of 2012; just one month. It stated that during that month there were ninety-four minors aged between thirteen and seventeen involved in prostitution in one form or another. That, Mr. Starke, is only part of what we're dealing with; it's only the tip of the iceberg."

She flipped through her notes.

"The trafficking you are concerned with is quite another story.... Hmmm, maybe I should try to explain the difference. Prostitution is generally a choice. The woman, for one reason or another, decides she can make a living selling her body so she hits the streets and does just that, *by choice*. Trafficking is when a woman is forced to sell her body. It's a little more complicated than that, but...."

She opened her iPad, flipped through several screens. "Let me read to you the official definition of human trafficking. 'The Palermo Protocols adopted by the U.N. General Assembly in 2000 define

162

human trafficking as the recruitment, transportation, transfer, harboring or receipt of persons, by means of the threat or use of force or other forms of coercion, of abduction, of fraud, of deception, of the abuse of power or of a position of vulnerability or of the giving or receiving of payments or benefits to achieve the consent of a person having control over another person, for the purpose of exploitation.' It's all about force, coercion, and fraud, Mr. Starke.... Can I get a drink of water?"

"Yes, of course." I got up and went out to get her a bottle from the refrigerator. I remembered those kids in the Dickersons' community room. I was sure he had more than the few we saw there. *Where the hell are they?*

I handed her the bottle, she took a sip, and then continued.

"Unfortunately, human trafficking is something most people don't hear much about, especially in a small city like this one, but it's becoming more of a problem, even here in Chattanooga. It's about children, enslaved, held against their will, forced into prostitution and hard labor. The pimps use a variety of brainwashing techniques to keep the kids under their control. Often, they are literally branded or tattooed to show they are owned, and by whom. If you believe it can't happen here, you're wrong,"

She took another sip of water. I leaned back in my chair. The more I thought about it, the angrier I became.

"Human traffickers often have stables of a dozen, maybe even as many as twenty girls. Does that sound familiar, Mr. Starke?"

I knew she was alluding to the Dickersons. I nodded, but I didn't answer.

"The johns are looking for new experiences, so the procurers, traffickers, pimps, whatever you want to call them, are looking for younger and younger children for their stables, and there are plenty of them on the streets. Some are kids who have run away from abusive homes, and some are enticed to leave "good" homes by promises of money, a fun job or an exciting time. Still others, as I mentioned before, are rented out as prostitutes, or even *sold* into sex slavery by their own parents, most of whom are either addicted to drugs or economically challenged."

"You say sold," Bob said. "What kind of money are we talking about?"

"It depends. Could be anywhere from $500 to $5,000, even more; usually, though, it's closer to the low end of the range, unless it's a trade sale, between one pimp and another. Then, depending upon the girl... well, you get the idea."

"So just how prevalent is it here?" I asked.

164

"As of right now, it's hard to tell, but to give you an idea, last month alone we rescued seven minors aged between thirteen and seventeen. How many are there out there today? God only knows; hundreds, perhaps."

I couldn't believe what I was hearing. "How can that be?"

"I'll give you an example," she said. "Two weeks ago, we took in a fifteen-year-old girl. She was in bad shape, addicted and infected with syphilis. I asked her how she became a prostitute. 'I just... met someone,' she said. That was it. She wouldn't explain who that someone was, or how she met him or her; that's right, we don't even know that. She wouldn't say another word."

She looked down at her iPad, flipped through a few screens, flipped back again, and then looked up at me.

"Romeo pimps," she said. "Those 'someones' are often handsome young men, even young boys. They target vulnerable girls and women in places like bus stops, malls and... online.... The hidden Internet is a huge driver of trafficking. When you've got a minute, check out a site called Back Page. Anyway, the Romeo is caring, loving, romantic, until he has them hooked, and then he will brainwash and isolate his victims. They are nasty, sadistic bastards, and there are more of them out there than we can handle."

She sat back, shook her head, obviously upset, took a drink of water, set the bottle down, and looked around the table.

I thought about Darius Willett.

"What else?" she asked, though I was sure she didn't want an answer.

"So you think the Dickersons are trafficking?" I asked.

She shrugged, didn't answer.

"What happens to the kids you rescue?" Kate asked.

"We hand them over to DCS. They try to place them with groups like the Draycotts', but they have only limited capacity. Some we send home, if we think the parents can handle it. Some run away again, go back to their pimps."

She paused, thought for a moment, and then continued.

"Look, what you don't understand, what most privileged folks don't understand, is that many of these kids come from abusive families. They are often treated better by their pimps than they were at home. They're used to being treated badly. It's their norm, their baseline; they expect nothing more."

166

She looked at Kate, then at me. "Does that help?"

I nodded, sighed. I suddenly felt very depressed.

"Let's go, Lieutenant," she said, rising to her feet. "I have a full schedule. Mr. Starke. If I can help, I will." She handed me her card. "Please, don't hesitate to call me. I would also ask that you keep me in the loop with your investigation. Good luck to you, sir. Get some bad guys for me, yeah?"

"Geeze," I said to Bob after they had left. "Who the hell would have thought it?"

"All the more reason we take down De Luca," he said. "Him and Dickerson."

"What about the Draycotts?"

"I think they are probably legit. The PD and DCS wouldn't use them if they weren't."

I nodded, turned to Tim, and said, "She mentioned a website called the Back Page. Have you heard of it?"

"Yeah, and Back Door, and a whole bunch more, but if you really want to dig into the murky depths of the Internet, you go to the Dark Web. You can find just about anything you want there."

"The Dark Web? What the hell is that?" I asked.

"The Dark Web, some folks call it the Deep Web, and they would be wrong, because the two are different. The Dark Web is a term used to describe areas on the Internet that can be accessed only through a specialized routing protocol with built-in encryption, an encrypted network that provides anonymity for the user; it hides your IP address, whereas the Deep Web is simply the content of databases and other web services that for one reason or another cannot be indexed by conventional search engines. For example, any website that requires you to log in is part of the Deep Web; your bank, for instance, or credit card company. The Dark Web can only be accessed using a... let's call it a special browser. It can be a wild and untamed world where the dreaded hackers prowl, looking for victims. I jest, of course, but you do have to be careful. It's not a place for the faint hearted."

"Do you... go there?"

He laughed. "Of course. That's what you pay me for."

I stared at him. *Now I really have something to think about.*

I looked at my watch. It was after five and I needed to get back to Amanda. I also had a lot of thinking to do.

I wrapped things up, sent everyone home for the weekend, waited until they'd all left the building, set the new security system, and went out to my car. By that time it was after six o'clock and dark outside. I looked at the new gate and smiled. It was quite a piece of equipment: some sixteen feet wide, set in a track and on wheels. A click of the remote and it slid slowly open. I drove out, stopped, clicked the remote and watched as it closed. It settled into the recessed steel jamb that was now attached to the wall of the building. The two steel bolts clicked solidly into place, effectively locking the gate shut. The gate had turned itself into a tempered steel fence. *Now that's what I'm talking about.*

I called Amanda and told her I was on the way. She said she had dinner ready, but that I needed to stop and get some wine. *Hmmm. I think I'm going to like having her around.*

I'm not quite sure how to explain my feelings when I arrived home that night. For sure I was a little uneasy. A dedicated bachelor, I was unused to the domestic bliss that confronted me when I walked in the door.

The table was laid with a white linen cloth and candles for God's sake, and there was no doubt that the lady could cook. She'd made a classic, Southern-style steak and gravy, and it *was* just like my mother used to make; she'd even made an apple pie. *Geeze!*

I showered, dressed, joined her in the dining room, and she handed me a cut glass tumbler with three fingers of Laphroaig Quarter Cask scotch with a single ice cube, no water. *Oh hell, this is too much.*

"Harry. You're very quiet. What's wrong?"

"Ummm, nothing. It's been a tough day."

"You want to talk about it?"

"Later... maybe. Right now I need to relax. Amanda?"

She looked at me across the table, worried. "Yes, Harry. What is it?"

"Look, I don't know how to say this... but... well, I'm not used to this, this, domesticity; it's not me. I'm not used to it. I need my space, space to relax, to think. I didn't think...."

She reached across the table, took my hand, and said, "I know. I'm sorry. I just thought that... well, our first night, and all. I'll keep myself to myself in the future. Maybe I can go home soon."

I looked at her, sighed, and shook my head. *Harry, you can be such a shit sometimes.*

I squeezed her hand. "No. That's not what I want. Just give me a little time to adapt, okay? It's nice having you here. In fact, I love it. Now, let's eat, and then I'll fill you in."

She gave me one of those cute little smiles and said, "Yes, please." I knew she wasn't talking about information.

Chapter 18

The following morning, we woke early. Well, I did. In fact, I didn't sleep much at all that night. I had too much on my mind. I watched the clock as the hours rolled by. Tick tock: visions of dead bodies, dirty little girls on street corners, little girls who might have stepped right out of a Dickens novel. Only Fagin was missing.... De Luca, Sam Draycott, Billy Dickerson all haunted my subconscious. I awoke in a cold sweat a little before five o'clock, sat up, and looked down at Amanda. She was breathing gently.

"Go back to sleep, Harry. It's too early." She didn't even open an eye.

I got out of bed, made coffee, set a cup on the nightstand beside her, went into the living room, sat down on the sofa and stared out at the river. It was still pitch dark, but the lights on the Thrasher Bridge glittered on the surface of the quiet waters. One by one, high atop the vast black bulk of Lookout Mountain, the lights came on, but I saw none of it. My mind was in a turmoil.

"Hey, lighten up," she said, as she snuggled up beside me. "It may never happen."

I put my arm around her, sipped on my coffee, stared out into the darkness, and said nothing.

It must have been thirty minutes later when she stirred, looked up at me and said, "What are we going to do, Harry? This is a nightmare."

I didn't answer. I couldn't, because I didn't know.

Kate called around nine o'clock. She was in a weird mood, wanted to come over and talk about the second body.

I looked at Amanda. "Kate wants to come visit, talk shop. You okay with that?"

She rolled her eyes. "Why wouldn't I be? I know her almost as well as I know you. Tell her to come on."

Kate arrived some thirty minutes later, dressed to kill. *Women!*

She said hi to Amanda, gave her a peck on the cheek, threw her coat down on the couch and hoisted herself up onto one of the bar stools. I have to tell you, I wasn't at all comfortable having these two together in my home, but....

She waited while I got a fresh cup of coffee. Amanda climbed onto the stool next to her. I joined them, took a stool opposite.

"Doc Sheddon says the body is male, probably seventeen or eighteen years old. There's not much left but the bones. He was clothed when he went into the drain, but most of what he was wearing has

173

rotted away. The teeth are all in good condition; no dental work, and there's a crack in the back of the skull, probably the result of a heavy blow. Sheddon says it's probably what killed him. There are no other obvious injuries. He also said that the body could have been put down there around the same time as the first one went under the boards."

"So they could be connected," I said.

She shrugged. "Possibly." She looked at Amanda. "Do you have anything on either the Draycotts or the Dickersons?"

"I know that the Draycotts do good work. They are very well thought of in the community. Ellen Draycott sits on the boards of several charitable organizations. She also runs a small, exclusive private practice. She caters to the rich and neurotic of our fair city; charges a fortune, so I'm told. All I know about the Dickersons is that he's been in trouble for as long as I can remember, but there's been nothing untoward these last few years."

"Harry," Kate said. "I'm really worried about this De Luca thing. I have a nasty feeling someone is either going to get badly hurt or killed. No. Let me finish. I also know you, and I know you're not just going to sit there and let it happen, and that really worries me. I'm also worried that Bob is going to take things into his own hands. I saw that look on his face. He worships you, and he's not going to let De Luca harm you. I understand how he feels, but I can't go along with it. You know that. I'm a cop. I have to enforce the law. If either one of you steps over the line...." She looked at me and then at Amanda. "I'll do it. I'll take you in. I'll have no choice."

"So that's really what you wanted to talk to me about?"

She nodded.

"I understand. I've already warned Bob. I can handle him. Now you also have to understand something. If anyone close to me, and that includes you, and even Lonnie, is hurt by De Luca... well, I'll say no more."

She left five minutes later. She wasn't happy, and neither was I. Even the usually upbeat Amanda looked somber.

The rest of the weekend passed uneventfully. Amanda and I stayed home, except for Sunday when we had lunch at the club with my father.

Chapter 19

On Monday morning, I left Amanda alone at the condo on Lakeshore Lane and headed in to the office. I wasn't the first to arrive. Jacque, Tim and Samantha were already there. I grabbed a cup of coffee, listened to a couple of messages, made a phone call and then went to check on Sam. The work was coming along, but she wouldn't let me see it. *So much for artistic temperament.*

The day went by quietly enough. I managed to get through a load of work, took Bob and Heather to lunch, met with a couple of potential clients, both lawyers, and then I figured it was time to check on Sam once more.

The door to the back office was open, and I could see her; she was wearing a white lab coat. She was seated at the desk with her back to the door, the reconstruction in front of her.

"Hey, Mr. Starke," she said, turning in her seat to look at me. "What do you think?" She rolled herself away from the desk. I took a sharp breath. *Oh wow!*

"Whew! That's amazing," I said.

She smiled. "I'm glad you like it."

"You think this is her?" I asked, as I crouched down in front of the bust. It was so lifelike. The girl

176

looked younger than I thought she would. I didn't put her any older than about sixteen. She wasn't beautiful, attractive, yes. Her face was slightly pear-shaped, the chin small and pointed, the cheeks high and chubby, the eyes slightly too narrow, and the nose slightly squashed. The lips were more Caucasian than African-American.

"She's mixed race," I said.

Samantha nodded. "Yes, I think so."

"Well done, Sam. Great job. Just hang on for a minute."

I went out into the main office and called the gang to take a look. They did. I stood at the rear of the group and watched. They were quiet. I understood why. It was like looking back in time; it was sobering to think about the young life, to wonder what dreams she might have had, and it was also deeply depressing.

I took photos of her with my iPhone. I had Tim take some with one of the company Nikons and had him print copies. I called Kate and invited her to come by and take a look. She arrived less than thirty minutes later. She looked at the girl, dumbfounded. Yes, it was no longer possible to think of her as an "it."

"I need to get photos out to all of the agencies," she said. "Maybe we'll get lucky and hit one of the missing persons flags. It's a long shot, but who knows?"

I nodded, and while she was talking, I emailed a copy to Amanda with a request she get it out on the six o'clock and late night news. I had an answer back almost immediately. Her new director had scheduled her to do the presentation herself. *Hell, so much for vacation time.*

I called her. "Sorry, Harry," she said. "I thought it was something I should do myself. I've also sent copies to the other stations; they've agreed to run the photo, too. Exposure. It's what we need. If you can run me by the station and wait for me, I should be no more than thirty minutes. They'll record the broadcast and run it again at eleven."

I looked at my watch. It was already after five. *Damnit.*

"Okay, get yourself ready. I'll be there in twenty minutes." In twenty minutes, she was ready and waiting; even her hair was done. She was wearing a black skirt, black turtle neck sweater, a scarlet blazer, and black ankle boots with low heels. It was a powerful look, calculated to grab attention.

We arrived at Channel 7 just as the six o'clock news was about to go on the air. She took her place in front of the array of flat-screen monitors and waited for the anchor to introduce her. When he did, she wasted no time. She went straight into a description of when, where and how the body had been found, and by whom. She also mentioned that Kate was running the investigation, and that I had been called in to consult. *Sheesh, more notoriety that I don't need.*

She gave a little background about Hill House, its history, and so forth, and then she introduced the photograph. It came up on one of the big screens behind her. At some three times life-size, the impact of the image was stunning. Samantha really had done a terrific job. Amanda went on to describe the girl, which wasn't easy, because no one had actually seen her. Nevertheless, by the time she'd finished, even I could see the slight young woman of mixed race. Amanda was a pro. She wrapped up by giving the usual contact information there and then; she did not send her viewers to the Channel 7 website. *Her boss is not going to be happy about that.*

She walked off the set, said her goodbyes, linked her arm in mine, and almost dragged me out of the building.

"Harry," she said. "I need a double vodka and a steak, in that order, and I don't want it home-cooked. Let's go to Porter's."

I knew Porter's well. It's located in the Read House, downtown. I was good with the choice,

179

mainly because the hotel offers valet parking. *Yes, I know. If anyone's going to get blown up, it should be me, not the parking staff. Oh yeah? Well, maybe you'd like to take my place.*

We arrived outside the hotel and I turned the Explorer over to the valets.

We waited to be seated. I felt like a goddamn mannequin. I hate being out in public with Amanda. Everyone knows her and, sure enough, every eye in the room turned to look at her. Several people raised their hands to say hello to her; one man even got to his feet and walked over and hugged her. When he was finished whispering in her ear, he stepped back, looked at me, shrugged, smiled, and held out his hand for me to shake.

"Sorry old chap," he said. *The damn fool is English. Might have known.*

"Hawkins," he continued. "Eric Hawkins. Mail on Sunday. I was just asking Amanda if you'd like to join—"

"Not tonight, Eric. Harry and I have work to do. Maybe another time?"

"Of course. You have my card. Give me a call. We'll do lunch."

"Gi' me a cawl," I mimicked, as he walked away. "We'll do lonch."

I received a swift, not-so-soft dig in the ribs from Amanda's elbow. "Be quiet, Harry. He'll hear you."

"So what? Damn poser. What's he to you anyway?" *Oh hell, here it comes.*

"Why, Harry," she said, as we followed the receptionist to our table, "I do believe you're jealous."

"Jealous my.... Who the hell is he?"

"He's a friend. A foreign correspondent. He works for one of the London Sunday newspapers. I met him through work. He's asked me out a couple of times, but I said no. I wonder who that woman is he's with. Bit of a skank."

"Hell, Amanda. Now who's jealous?"

"You are, sweetie, but I'll make it up to you. I promise. Now, please order for me, and *do not* spare the calories."

"The lady," I said to the waiter, "will have a filet mi.... Hey! What?" She'd kicked me under the table. She smiled sweetly at me. I got the message.

"The lady will have the whiskey glazed T-Bone." I looked at her. She nodded, still smiling. "With everything. I'll have the filet. We'll both have french onion soup, and we'll split an order of crab cakes. For the wine.... we'll have a bottle of Chateau St Michelle." *Not the most expensive bottle on the list, but what the hell; it's only Monday.*

181

I was being facetious when I ordered the steak for her. Never in a million years did I think she could manage everything. She proved me wrong. The steak disappeared in short order, followed by a healthy portion of hot toddy cheesecake. *The woman's a... a.... I jest. She has... a healthy appetite. Yeah, that's it.*

We finished up and I paid the bill. I looked at my watch. It was eight-thirty.

The valet brought the car to front and opened the door for Amanda. *So far, so good.*

It was a nice evening. The air was crisp, the sky clear, and there was a three-quarter moon over the silhouette of Lookout Mountain. I drove back to my place, along 153, over the Thrasher Bridge and took the Lake Resort Drive exit. I turned onto Lakeshore Lane and....

"Something's not right. I can feel it. That car parked next door. It doesn't belong to them, and they're away in the Bahamas for Christmas. Keep your head down."

I drove on past, fast. I tried to get a look inside the car, and at my front doors, garage and house, but it was just a blur: nothing.

"Goddamnit!"

I turned into a driveway 200 yards on and then reversed out again, and drove back toward my condo. I was just in time to see the tail lights disappearing around the bend. I hit the gas pedal, but the Explorer is no Maxima. It surged forward like a boat in a gale.

"Damnit!"

They, if it was a they, were gone. Now what?

I parked the car on the road, fifty yards from the condo, and hit the remote garage door opener. Nothing. Too far.

"Damnit!"

I got out of the car, walked a few steps, and pushed the button. This time the door rolled smoothly up.

"Stay in the car," I said. What I should have said was, 'get out of the car,' because she did the exact opposite; she got out of the car.

"Stay here... oh hell, never mind. Come on, but stay back."

I checked around the garage door opening, and then the front door. All seemed to be in order. The security alarm had not been triggered, so....

"Follow me," I said. She did. She followed me in through the garage and up the stairs in the kitchen.

"Sit down. Give me a minute. I want to check the recorder."

One of the cameras at the front had caught the car arriving, just minutes before we did. I watched. It sat there. No one left it. I saw my car arrive, and the quick reverse as the black BMW Series 5 sedan rocketed away toward Lake Resort Drive. Obviously, the intention had not been to do harm, but instill a sense of terror, and by God, it had worked.

When I joined her on the sofa, Amanda's face was a picture. She was pale; not a hint of a smile.

"What are we going to do, Harry? We can't go on like this. Not for long, anyway."

"I dunno. I have to put a stop to it; that's for sure, but how? Short of killing him, I have no idea. Might just come to that...."

"Ooh, no. He might kill you."

"Hey. You think? He's not good enough." I was less confident than I sounded, and I said it only for Amanda's benefit.

"You still have the Glock in your pocketbook?"

"Yes, but I don't know if...."

"No, don't know if," I said. "It's not likely to happen but..." I took her chin in my fingers and turned her face toward me. "You have any doubts, any at all. You don't give 'em a chance. You shoot first. You got that?"

She nodded, put her arms around my neck, and pulled me in close. "Damn you, Harry Starke," she whispered.

I knew exactly what she meant.

Chapter 20

Before I left home the next morning, I removed the flash drive from my security system and replaced it. When I viewed it the previous evening, I couldn't see the license plate on the Beemer; it was too dark, but maybe Tim could make something of it.

Once again, it had been a night of little sleep. Amanda had been restless, squirming, kicking, flailing. In the end, I had to get up. I lay down on the sofa and dozed, and dreamed.

Once I arrived at the office, things became a little cleared. I knew I had some serious thinking to do, about the De Luca situation, but I also knew I had to go see both the Draycotts and the Dickersons. I also had a plan that might help me figure out some other things. I wanted to know about trafficking in Chattanooga. I already knew it was happening, but I wanted to know who, how and where. I needed to pay Benny Hinkle a visit.

I also wanted to know who the hell had parked next door to my condo last night.

I punched the button on the house phone. "Bob, we need to talk. Grab a coffee and come on in."

I gave him a quick rundown on the events of the previous evening and asked for suggestions.

"Do you have any idea who it might have been?" he asked.

"No. It was a black series 5 BMW four-door. The security camera caught it, but it was too dark for it to get the plate."

"So. It could have been anybody: Dickerson's people, maybe, but it's more likely they were De Luca's."

"I don't know, but we have to put a stop to it, somehow. Yeah, I know. You want to kill his ass. Forget it, Bob. I'm not going to spend the rest of my days in the can for that piece of garbage. We need to come up with something else. Has Tim said anything about the dead girl? We need to know who she was."

"Not to me. He was tapping away like a fiend last time I looked. You want me to get him?"

"No. I'll do it." I punched the button.

"Tim," I said, as he sat down, iPad in hand. "What have you been able to find out about the dead girl? Have you found anything?"

"Yeah, quite a lot. In fact, I think I may have found her. In all, I got a total of six hits on NamUS, but only one of them looked promising. Heather has been taking calls all morning, the result of Amanda's broadcasts the previous evening, but so far she's heard nothing that got her excited."

He looked at his iPad, flipping through one screen after another, pausing now and then, clicking his tongue against his top pallet. *Damn, that boy can be annoying.*

"Tim!" I said, sharply. "Are you going to tell us or not?"

"Yeah, of course. Here she is." He handed me his iPad. I looked at the photo; I was stunned. I picked up the photo of the reconstruction and held it side-by-side with the one on the iPad. *It could be. It just could be.*

I looked at Tim. He was grinning. I handed the iPad and photo to Bob. For several seconds, he looked back and forth between the two, then slowly nodded, handed the pad back to Tim, and looked across the desk at me.

"It's her," he said.

"Okay, Tim," I said. "Let's have it."

"Her name, if it's her, was Brinique Williams. Her father is white, her mother is African-American, Bahamian. She ran away from her home in Greenville, North Carolina, in May of 2005. She would have been seventeen the following November. She called her mother once, a week after she left home. Told them she was okay, that she'd met someone, and they were not to worry about her. According to the NamUS listing, she has an old injury to her left wrist and... fillings in teeth numbers thirteen and fifteen. I think it's her. I've run the name through all of the relevant data bases, but other than the NamUS listing, I got nothing. The girl, as far as the records go, left the planet not long after she left home."

"Wow, good work, Tim," I said. "Do we have contact information for the parents? I'll go see them. See if we can't get confirmation."

"Ummm...." Tim hesitated. "I hope I didn't do a bad thing, but I already called them. They are coming down, today. They are bringing dental records, photos.... They'll be here around two o'clock... sorry."

"Nothing to be sorry about, son. You saved me the trouble is all." I looked at my watch. It was already after eleven.

"Okay, I need a few minutes. They're coming here, right?"

Tim nodded, already getting to his feet, as was Bob.

"One more thing," I said to Tim. "Take a look at the video on this." I tossed the flash card from my home security system to him. "I need the license plate number." It was a forlorn hope, but maybe I'd get lucky.

"Bob, I need you to be thinking about what we discussed earlier. Yes?"

He said he'd give it some thought, and then followed Tim out into the main office. I picked up the phone and called Kate.

"We have her," I said, when she picked up. "At least I think we do."

"And good morning to you, too," she said. "You have who?"

"The girl; the dead girl; we got a hit, and a tentative ID. The parents are on their way here. They'll be here around two. You need to be here too, yeah?"

"Whew, you need to slow down," she said. "Yes, I'll be there. Who is she?"

I filled her in on the details and then called Amanda and told her I was on my way to pick her up for lunch.

Chapter 21

Kate was already there when Michael and Dondra Williams walked in through the front door just before two-fifteen. He was a big man, heavy, overweight, balding, maybe fifty-two or fifty-three years old. She was petite, several years younger, and still quite beautiful, though it was easy to see that years of sorrow had jaded her looks.

I ushered them into my office, beckoned for Kate and Amanda to join us, and then I closed the door. They sat together on the sofa. Kate and Amanda took the two chairs. I brought up one of high-back chairs from in front of my desk.

"Pretty tree," Dondra said, distractedly, nodding in the direction of Jacque's vast creation in the corner of the room. "Ours is not quite as big...." She trailed off, looked at me, her eyes wide. I felt like shit.

"I'm sorry you had to come all this way," I said. "I know you'll understand when I say I hope it was a wasted journey."

They both nodded.

"I have something I want to show you. I hope it won't be too much of a shock. Are you ready?"

Before they'd arrived, I'd had the reconstruction moved to my office and placed on the coffee table facing the sofa. It was covered with a white cloth.

For several moments, I hesitated, almost to the point it must have appeared I was trying to create drama; I wasn't. I just was beyond apprehensive. Finally, I took a deep breath and pulled the cloth from the head.

"Ohhh!" Dondra gasped, then slipped off the sofa onto her knees, her hands reaching for her face. Michael grabbed her arm, slipped to the floor beside her, put his arm around her, and pulled her in close. She was now in tears. There was no need to ask the question; the answer was already obvious: we were looking at the recreation of Brinique Williams.

It took them both a while to get themselves together. I left the room. Kate and Amanda stayed to offer a little comfort and support. *How the hell do you comfort someone when you've just dropped a bomb like that on them?*

I looked at my watch. It was still only two-thirty. *Hell, I need a little comfort myself.*

I went to the cupboard in the back office and grabbed the unopened bottle of Laphroaig, looked at it, shook my head, and put it back. Now was not the time to indulge myself.

"Harry. Can you come, please?" Amanda leaned out of the half-open door to my office, saw me, and came the rest of the way out.

"I think they're ready to talk," she whispered. "The woman is in a hell of a state, but he seems composed enough."

"What happened to her?" Williams asked. "Did she... did... she suffer?" *What the hell do you say to that? Of course she suffered. She was strangled, damnit.*

Dondra was sobbing quietly. I looked at Kate, my eyebrows raised. She nodded, and said, "No, she didn't. It would have been very quick." *It was a lie, but forgivable.*

We talked for more than an hour. It seemed the kid wasn't at all bad, at least according to them. She ran a solid B plus in high school, played soccer, went to church... and then.... *Yeah, you guessed it. She met a boy.*

From that point on, it was all downhill. The grades dropped, she stopped talking to her parents, stayed out late, wouldn't tell them where she'd been, and then they'd found the pills. Mollies, is what they'd been told they were, a form of ecstasy. They locked her in her room, tried to get her to tell them where they came from, but she wouldn't talk. She refused to eat, even drink. They panicked, decided to take her to a doctor. That was on May 27, 2005, a Friday. Unfortunately, the minute they were outside the front door, she bolted. Other than that single phone call a week later on Saturday June 4, they'd heard nothing from her since. No, she didn't say where she was, who she was with, or what she was doing.

I showed them photos of the necklace and the ring. The necklace they'd never seen before. The ring had belonged to the boy. An African-American kid named Ricky Jessell, RJ.

"How old was he?" Kate asked.

"I think he was nineteen," Dondra said. "We thought he was too old for her, but you know how kids are. They never listen to their parents."

"Did you ever meet him?" Kate asked.

They both shook their heads. I asked if he was still around. They said they'd looked for him, but he disappeared the same time Brinique did. Why wasn't I surprised to hear that? *I wonder....*

"How about his parents, relatives?" I asked.

"As far as we know," Michael said, "he had none, they were dead, his parents. I don't think he had any brothers and sisters, at least we couldn't find any. He seemed to be all alone."

There wasn't a whole lot more we could do for them, nor they for us.

"Tim said you had some photographs," I said.

Williams nodded and handed me a large envelope. Inside were a half-dozen color photos of the girl, and her dental records. I leafed through them, not saying a word. I couldn't. I handed them off to Kate; she, in turn, handed them to Amanda.

"Can you get one of these on the air this evening, with a request for information?" she asked her.

Amanda said she would, and then handed the photos back to me. I took them out to Tim and asked him to scan them into the system and then print copies for everyone, including Amanda. That done, I gave the originals back to the Williams.

I asked if they had somewhere to stay. Dondra replied by asking if it would be possible to see her daughter.

"Do I need to identify her?" she asked.

"No. I don't think that would be a good idea," Kate said. "She's been gone a long time, and there's not much to see. I think it would be best if you remembered her as she was. I will, however, need DNA samples from you both. We'll use them and... well, we'll use them and her dental records to confirm the identity, but I don't think that there's much doubt: it's Brinique."

"How... how do you do that?" Dondra asked.

"I'll take mouth swabs from you both."

"Yes, I know that, but how about Brinique? You say there's not much left of her."

I looked at Kate. I could see she didn't know what to say. She stood. "I'll be just a minute. I need to get the kits from the car." Dondra nodded, and Kate left to get them.

"So," I said. "You didn't say if you have somewhere to stay tonight?"

"We're not staying. We'll drive back home tonight. When can we have... her? We need to lay her to rest."

"I'll let you know as soon as I know. I'll try to hurry it up. I'll call you."

Fifteen minutes later, they were gone, and I felt like shit. It's always the same. Parents try so hard to be brave, but they never can. *How do you cope with something like that?*

I walked them to the door, watched them go, and then returned to my office where Kate and Amanda were talking together. They both rose to their feet when I entered.

"I have to get back to the PD," Kate said. "What are your plans, Harry?"

"We need to visit both the Dickersons and the Draycotts. Are you up for it?"

"Of course, but when? I can't do it today."

"It needs to be soon. Tomorrow is our last day here before we close the office for Christmas. I'll call

196

Judge Strange and see if he'll issue warrants. If I can, will you or Lonnie go pick them up?"

"Yeah, I'll have Lonnie do it. I'll pick you up tomorrow morning, around nine-thirty. Be ready. Amanda, don't take any shit from him, okay?" *What the hell was that about?*

"What did she mean by that?" I asked, when Kate had left.

"Just girl talk," she said with a grin. "She knows you too well, Harry. I hope I get to know you that well, too."

"The hell you do," I said. I wasn't quite sure what was going on, and I was even less sure I liked it.

"Harry, I need to run these photos by the station. Can we do that, like now?"

"Yes, we can do that, but first I need to have a word with Tim, make a phone call, and then I have something I want to do before Kate and I go visiting tomorrow. I can take you by the station and then I can either leave you there for an hour, or you can come with me. Which do you prefer?"

"It depends. What is it you want to do?"

"I need to drop by the Sorbonne and talk to Benny Hinkle, find out what he knows about prostitution and trafficking in the town. If anybody can fill me in, it will be him. You wanna go with me or not?"

She thought for a minute, then nodded. "I do, but first let's get these photos and the girl's name on the air. Maybe we'll get lucky. Maybe someone will recognize her. The station is only a couple of miles from downtown. It won't take long."

"Okay, but we can't hang about yacking. I need to get there early, before the bar get busy."

"Yacking? I'll punish you for that," she hissed. *Hmmm, the night holds promise.*

I asked Tim to see what he could find on Ricky Jessell. I figured he might just be the key to this thing.

I called Judge Strange, told him what we needed, and that Lonnie would be by to pick them up. He didn't even ask why I needed them.

I've always said, it's not what you know, it's who you know, and this was one of those times when it paid off big. Judge Strange owed me a favor, one he could never repay. I'd found his wayward, drug-addicted daughter for him, and brought her home. Warrants were nothing, after that.

Chapter 22

It was just after four-thirty that afternoon when I parked the Explorer on a meter on Market Street. I figured there were enough people, mostly tourists, milling around that it would be safe enough from… well, you know. Amanda slipped her arm through mine and we made the short walk from there to the Sorbonne, maybe two minutes.

"What's he like, Benny Hinkle?" she asked, as we walked.

I smiled at her. "You'll see. He's a complex character, hard to define." *Whew! Is that an understatement, or what?*

The place was already open, but there were no customers, which was unusual. Even so, the mind-numbing music reverberated off the walls. I parked myself on a stool at the bar. Amanda hoisted herself up onto the one next to it.

"There he is," I said.

Benny was at the far end of the bar, his back toward me; he was talking animatedly to Laura, his partner and bartender. She saw me over his shoulder, dipped her head, and whispered something to Benny. He stiffened, turned slowly around, looked disgusted, threw the wet bar towel into the sink, and shambled toward me, shaking his head.

"Damn it, Starke. I thought I told you to stay away from me, stay outa my bar. Who's the tail?"

Amanda snorted, trying not to laugh.

"Now, Benny. Is that any way to greet an old friend?"

"Old friend, my ass. You are bad news, Starke. Every time you come in here, I get hurt. Now go on. Get outa here.... How come I ain't seen you in here before, miss?"

"Amanda Cole. Nice to meet you, Benny."

"Amanda... Amanda... Cole. Awe hell. I thought the face was familiar. You're that broad from Channel 7. Harry, I don't need this shit. You gotta get outa here the both of you. NOW!"

"Benny, I need some info. I already owe you one. If you hadn't warned me about De Luca.... Well, you did. Now...."

"Not now, damn it. They was back last night, wantin' to know if you'd been in. I told 'em no, but I ain't sure they b'lieved me. I can't do it, Starke. You have to go... *please.*"

I almost felt sorry for him. "Benny, I'm not going anywhere until you tell me what I need to know. So, let's talk. The quicker you spill it, the quicker I'm out of here."

He glared at me, then Amanda, looked furtively around, at the front door, licked his lips, nodded, and said, "Okay, but be quick about it."

"Turn that damn noise down first." He did.

"Billy Dickerson," I said "is running some sort of home for kids on Cherry. It's just a couple of blocks or so from here. What do you know about it?"

He took a deep breath. "Nothin', an' I don't wanna. Dickerson's a goddamn crook. I stay away from people like him."

"What about his kids, Benny? Is he pimping them out?"

He shook his head. "I told ya, I don't know nothin' about what he does. He has some very nasty people workin' for 'im and I stay outa his business."

"Tell me about them, his people."

"Oh, for Christ's sake, Harry. You're gonna get me in all kinds a shit." He turned and yelled over his shoulder, "Laura. C'mere."

Laura, as I said, is Benny's long-time partner. I'm not sure if it's a romantic or a monetary arrangement, although I suspect it's the latter. I shudder to think it might be the former. She's quite a character, the epitome of the stereotypical Southern barkeep, a big, blowsy bottle blonde, usually attired in a tank top that barely covers her oversize breasts, cut off jeans that barely cover her ass, and, for God's sake, cowboy boots. She wore little makeup. In fact, if you took her out of the Sorbonne, cleaned her and dressed her up a little, she wouldn't be a bad-looking woman.

"Hellooo, Harry," she said, as she cut me a look that could only have been taken as an invitation.

I caught Amanda's smile out of the corner of my eye.

"Cut it out, Laura," Benny growled. "He wants to know what we know about them freaks that work for Dickerson. You know more about 'em than I do; you serve 'em all the time."

She looked at me, then at Amanda. The smile was gone from her face. "You need to stay away from them, Harry. They're real nasty asses."

"Tell me."

She heaved a sigh, grabbed a glass from the back of the bar, jerked herself a beer, and swallowed half of it in one gulp.

"There are four of 'em. The main man is Darius Willett; they call him Romeo."

"Romeo? Why?" I asked.

"'Cause that's what he is, a Romeo."

I was pretty sure I knew why they called him that. "Go on," I said.

"Yeah, well, there's Darius. Then there's Mouse; that's Mickey Donavan. He's all muscle; don't talk much, just... well, he likes to 'flict pain, and he likes 'em young, his women, well, girls. An' there's Woody; don't know anything about him. He only comes in now and then. Then there's Little Jackie. I don't know his last name. He's Dickerson's driver, among other things, a goddamn sadist for one. Last, there's Lisa; don't know her name either, but she's Jackie's woman. They've all been comin' in here for a couple a years, or so. They spend big, tip well. That's it. That's all I know about 'em."

"Laura," I said. "What do you know about Dickerson? What's he up to?"

Her eyes shifted. She looked at Benny, then at the floor. I could tell she didn't want to talk about it.

"Tell 'im," Benny said.

Again, she heaved a huge breath. Her breasts seemed to inflate, and then collapse: it was unnerving.

"Look. I don't know, but I can guess. I've seen Darius in here with some of Sal De Luca's people, Gino for one, until you... well, you know, and Tony, always Tony. Sometimes Darius will bring a girl in. He ain't supposed to. They're all underage, an' I don't serve 'em, but the girls, they always look... I dunno, washed out?"

203

"What do you mean, washed out?" I asked.

"Washed out, you know... damn, Harry. I dunno. Like they ain't with us, spacey; spaced out. Shit. Use your imagination."

"You think they're running the girls, Laura? You think they're trafficking?"

"Hell yeah, I think they're runnin' them... I don't know for sure, but if I had to bet on it. Trafficking? I ain't real sure what that is, but yeah, that too, whatever it might be. If it involves girls, they're doin' it, I shouldn't wonder. Dickerson's a bad ass. He has access to 'em, girls, little girls. What do you think he'd be doing?"

"And you think De Luca...."

She started to back away. I could tell she didn't want to go any further. "Laura, I need to know. It's important. I'm investigating two murders, both of them young kids. One was stuffed under the floorboards of that old house up on McCallie, the other was jammed into the drains. I think Dickerson has something to do with both, and if he's in cahoots with De Luca."

She nodded, looked at Benny. He nodded.

"I can't say for sure, but Darius and Tony spend a lot of time over there, talking," she pointed to a corner in the darker regions of the bar, "about what I don't know, but you can tell it's serious. I tried to listen one time, but as soon as I got close, they clammed up, looked at me, and waited 'till I went away. One time, Darius brought a kid in here, a girl, maybe fourteen, fifteen years old. She left with Tony. You figure it out."

"Okay, Starke," Benny said. "You got what you wanted. Now get outa here, before they come an' find me talkin' to ya."

"Okay," I said. "I get it. Thanks, Benny, Laura; I owe you one, both of you."

"Yeah, you do," he growled. "That's two you owe me."

I got up off the stool, handed each of them one of my cards, and said, "Call me. You hear or see anything. You call me. Laura, you see any of them in here with a girl, I want to know. You call, ASAP. Yeah?"

She said she would, but I very much doubted it. De Luca was big trouble, and they both knew it, probably better than anyone. Benny had already fallen foul of Gino Polti, a one-time De Luca soldier, now dead, thanks to me. They both were well aware that to talk... well, that kind of trouble, I wouldn't wish on anyone. I remembered only too well what had happened to Marty Cassell and James Westwood. Cassell lived to tell about it; Westwood didn't.

When we left the Sorbonne it was a little after five o'clock. The car? I hoped it hadn't been touched. I took the expandable baton from my jacket pocket, flipped it open, squeezed the mirror into position on the tip, and walked slowly around the car, looking at the underside. Amanda watched, and she wasn't smiling. I felt so damned stupid, especially when I saw a kid, no more than six years old, also watching me. *I'm turning into a goddamn clown. De Luca would be absolutely delighted if he could see me.*

Exasperated, I looked at Amanda. "Move over there, away from the car."

She did as she was told, her face white. I grabbed the mirror, collapsed the baton, unlocked the car, threw both onto the rear seat, sat down heavily, punched the starter, got back out of the car, and looked around: no explosion, no ticking bomb, nothing. *Screw you, Sal. That was the last time. I'm gonna fix you, if it kills me.... Hah!*

Then I had another thought. I walked around to the passenger side, dropped into that seat, and got out again. Still no big bang. *Screw you, De Luca.*

I beckoned Amanda, held the door for her, told her I needed several stiff drinks and by six o'clock we were in the bar at the club. We had a few drinks, dinner, and then headed home to Lakeshore and enjoyed an uneventful evening, thank God.

But it wasn't all wine and roses. I was still mulling over all that Benny and Laura had said. I had De Luca on my mind, too. If he was up to what I thought he was, he wasn't going to allow me to screw it up for him. I had to stop that son of a bitch, and soon. But much worse than that, as I lay beside Amanda listening to her gentle breathing, I was haunted by the image of Brinique Williams. I still had no clue what had happened to her, or why, but I sure as hell was going to find out. And there was one more thing floating around in my head, Amanda. It had been five days since she'd moved in with me, and... well, I was beginning to like it. *Damn it.*

Chapter 23

At nine-fifteen the following morning, Wednesday, two days before Christmas, I was at my desk with a cup of Dark Italian Roast when Doc Sheddon called. He'd run the dental records. We didn't need to wait for a DNA match with her parents; the girl from Hill House was, indeed, Brinique Williams. It was no surprise, just heartbreaking.

Now we had to find out what the hell had happened to her.

I sat at my desk, the photos of the girl spread out in front of me. No she wasn't beautiful, but I thought that one day she might have been. She was pretty, and slim, but still too young to have developed into womanhood. *Bastard. How the hell could you do it? How could you bring yourself to kill this poor kid?*

For what must have been fifteen, maybe twenty minutes, I sat there, staring at the five photographs. *I'll get him,* I silently promised her, *and when I....* The thought was interrupted by a knock at the door.

"Yeah. Come on in."

The door opened, and Kate stuck her head in. "You ready to go?" She was armed with warrants for both the Draycotts and the Dickersons.

"Not quite. Come on in. Take a seat. You want coffee?"

"No, Harry. I have Lonnie waiting in the car, and I have six uniforms waiting at the Draycotts'. We need to go. By the way, it might be a good idea if Tim came with us. You never know what we might run into. Can we do that?"

"Yeah. Okay. Give me a minute. Let me get dressed." I buzzed Tim, told him to grab his gear, and then I put on my golf jacket, checked the rig and the nine under my left arm, and then climbed into my heavy coat.

Five minutes later, Tim and I were in the rear of the unmarked, and Lonnie was up front in the passenger seat. We were heading for the Clermont Foundation on East Brainerd Road.

They were not expecting us. Kate and I had learned early on in our law enforcement careers that the element of surprise is a mighty tool when carrying out a search warrant.

We pulled up outside the front of the building, the two cruisers in line behind us. I'd never been on the receiving end of such a visit, but I had a feeling it must be extremely intimidating.

Together, the four of us walked in through the front door, into the reception area. We were followed by two uniforms. The girl behind the desk smiled brightly up at us, until Kate informed her of the purpose of our visit. She picked up the phone and pushed a button.

"The police are here, Dr. Draycott. They have a search warrant.... Yes, I'll tell them." She put the phone down, looked up at us, her face serious.

"Doctor Draycott will be with you momentarily. If you would like to take a seat...."

"That's not how it works, I'm afraid," Kate said. "This warrant gives us free access to—"

The door behind the reception desk opened and Doctor Ellen walked through. She wasn't happy... ah, that would be putting it mildly. She was pissed.

"Mr. Starke. What are you doing here? Who are you and what do you want?" she said to Kate.

"I'm Lieutenant Catherine Gazzara, Major Crimes Unit. I have a warrant for your files. I need your records for the years 2004 and 2005, including the period of transition, when you took over from the Dickersons."

"Just a minute, I need to call my husband." She took phone from her lab coat pocket and punched in a text message.

"Now, Dr. Draycott. I need to see them now." Kate started forward toward the rear door.

"Wait!" It was almost a shout. "I'll take you."

And she did. We were met at the door of the room where the records were kept by Dr. Sam Draycott, and he was boiling.

"What the hell is the meaning of this? You can't come barging in here going through private patient records. It's unheard of."

"I don't want to see your medical records, Doctor," Kate said. "What I do want see are the personnel records of the young girls who found refuge here. I also want the personnel records of the staff you employed from 2004 through 2005, full time, part time, and volunteer. *All of them,* including those of the nine missing children. I will also need any files for missing males."

He looked at his wife. He obviously didn't know what to do. She shrugged.

"No medical records, Lieutenant," she said. "I will not allow you to see any of those. I can, however, show you the listings of the girls in residence at Hill House from when we took over. As you know, we took over from the Dickersons. There were twenty-two girls here then, and four boys. Seven of the girls went with him and so did two of the boys; the other fifteen stayed with us. We would have taken them all, but.... Well, the others wanted to go, so we let them."

She opened the door and stood aside for us to enter. The room was barely furnished, just a large table around which were spaced a half-dozen chairs, and a single row of filing cabinets along the back wall. There were also two computer monitors on the table.

"Everything was computerized just after we moved into this new building, but we still have the old hard copies. Which do you prefer?"

"Tim, you take the computer," I said. "Kate and I will take the hard copies."

Tim nodded, sat down, and started hammering the keys.

"How does he know what he's looking for?" Sam Draycott asked.

"Oh, he knows," I said. "He'll find stuff you didn't know you had."

The two Draycotts looked at each other. Sam looked even more worried than he had before.

It seemed only minutes before Tim looked around and asked where the towers were located.

"Towers?" Sam Draycott asked.

"The computers; the big boxes," Tim said.

"Oh those. They're in here." He opened the door to what once must have been a walk-in closet. The two towers were side-by-side on a shelf.

Tim nodded, inserted a thumb drive into one of them, went back to the table, hit the keyboard a couple of times, then turned and said, "All done," as he retrieved the thumb drive.

Kate and I were still on the first of the hard copies.

Tim took the one I was holding and flipped through it. "You don't need those. I already have them... *and a whole lot more,*" he whispered.

I looked at Kate; she looked at Tim. "You sure?" she asked.

"Oh yeah. I got it."

"Fine!" I said. "Go wait for us in the car. We'll be a few more minutes."

I waited until he'd left and then said to Kate, "I think it would be a good idea to take all of the relevant hard copies with us. There aren't a whole lot of them. Maybe fifty or sixty files. What do you think?"

She agreed, gave Lonnie instructions to remove and box the files, signed a receipt, and handed it to Ellen Draycott. The woman snatched it out of her hand, looked at it, and handed it her husband. She seemed about to say something, but she changed her mind, snapped her mouth shut, and glared at us.

Kate ignored the look and asked the Draycotts to sit. They did, but reluctantly. Kate and I sat down opposite them. Lonnie finished packing the records into two cardboard file boxes and stood with his back to the wall, his hands in his pockets.

"I have a few questions to ask of you both," Kate said, "if you don't mind."

"There's nothing more we can tell you," Ellen Draycott said. "2005 was a long time ago, almost eleven years, and we were just at the beginning of our mission then. We know nothing about the poor girl."

"It's not just the girl," Kate said. "We found a second body, a young man, or boy, in the drains. Nasty."

They looked at one another; both had gone two shades paler.

"Before we get into specifics," Kate said. "I need to know more about the transition from Dickerson to you. It appears to have taken place over a period of three months..." she looked at her iPad, "from June through August. Tell me about it."

"What's to tell?" Ellen Draycott said. "Dickerson lost his lease, and we took it over. There was, as you said, a transition period. We had the lease from June 13, but we couldn't make the move immediately.

214

Dickerson filled the gap. I was here by myself for the last two weeks of June. Until my husband was able to join me in mid-August, the Dickersons and I ran things at Hill House together. They left the first week in September, as I recall."

"I asked you this earlier, but let's do it one more time," Kate said. "What about the girls? How many were there, and what happened to them?"

"And I told you. There were twenty-two girls. We kept all but the seven who insisted on going with the Dickersons. You'll find that information noted in their files: those who stayed, and those who didn't. Oh, and if you're interested, we brought five of our own rescues to the house: three girls and two boys."

"Tell me what you know about Brinique Williams," I said, watching them both carefully. She didn't flinch. Him, I wasn't sure; tiny flicker of an eyelid, maybe? Maybe it was nothing.

"Who?" he said.

"Brinique Williams. She would have been almost seventeen back in August 2005 when you took over Hill House."

"Was she... was she the girl who... died?" he asked.

"She was," Kate said.

They were both shaking their heads.

215

"Maybe this will jog your memories," I said, reaching inside my coat pocket for the envelope. I placed a five by seven print of the girl on the table in front of them; I could have sworn Doctor Sam drew in a breath when he looked at it. Other than that, they were still, perhaps too still.

"I've never seen her before," Doctor Ellen said. "She certainly wasn't one of ours. Perhaps you should talk to the Dickersons." With that, she rose and walked out of the room.

"I... don't know her either," Sam Draycott said. "I... I have to go, too. I have much to do in time for the holiday. Please excuse me. If you don't mind. I have things to do." He rose from his seat and was about to follow his wife out of the room.

"One more thing before you go, Doctor," I said.

He slowly sat down again, his hands on the edge of the table.

"Does the name Ricky or Richard Jessell mean anything to you?" Again, there was the slightest twitch of his left eyelid.

He didn't hesitate. He shook his head, then said, "No. I don't know that name at all. Now, if you don't mind. I have things to do." Again, he rose from the table. This time we let him go.

I got up and followed him out. Kate and Lonnie followed me, Lonnie toting the file box. Tim was already inside the unmarked, waiting for us.

"So what do you think?" Kate said, as she pushed the starter.

"I'm liking Sam Draycott less and less," I said. "He gave the impression that he wanted to be helpful, but I think he was stonewalling. Did you notice how uncomfortable he was, especially when I showed him the photo and asked him about the boy? I think he was hiding something. Whether it has anything to do with the dead girl, I don't know. Hell, they could be hiding any number of things: embezzlement, Medicare fraud, you name it. I think he's a man of secrets. I also think she's the driving force, wears the pants. What do you think?"

"Yeah, I noticed the look on his face. He's good, but not quite good enough. As to Ellen Draycott, I don't like her, not one little bit. Harry, I need a favor."

"Sure, if I can."

"I want to use Tim for a couple of days, at the PD. Would you be okay with that?"

I looked at Tim; he grinned, nodded.

"Well, sure, but why not at my office?"

"I need the computer files, and those we removed from the Dickersons, searched inside the

217

PD, under strict supervision, likewise the hard copies. If there's anything in them, I don't want the evidence tainted."

"Makes sense, but—"

"Oh, don't worry," she interrupted. "You'll have access to everything through Tim. He can make copies. I'll have copies of the hard files made and sent to your office as soon as possible. I know you want to go through them yourself."

I nodded, somewhat bewildered.

"Okay, we all ready to head on over to Cherry Street?"

Chapter 24

We arrived at Cherry Street in a convoy, Kate's unmarked followed by the two cruisers. As before, both the side and rear doors were securely locked. Lonnie banged on the side door and we waited.

The door opened a crack, and Lonnie pushed it wide open, knocking the young girl sideways. I stepped forward and led the way along the corridor to the stairs.

"What's behind these doors, I wonder," Kate said, as we passed by them, three on either side. This time I noticed the security cameras, two in the corridor and one at the top of the stairs.

We were met by India Dickerson. I had to admit, she looked a whole lot better than she did the first time I met her. She was wearing a tight red turtleneck sweater and form-fitting black leather skirt.

"You again," she said. "Who are all these people?"

Kate didn't give me a chance to answer. She stepped forward, warrants in hand, and said, "I'm Lieutenant Gazzara, Chattanooga Police. I have a warrant to search your files. Please take me to them."

India looked down at the papers in Kate's hand, then up at her, then at me. She seemed about to say something, thought better of it, turned and walked to the desk. She picked up the phone, punched a button, and said, "The police are here, with a warrant. Get out here. Now!"

She put the phone down and turned to face us. "What's all this about? We told you, Mr. Starke, that we know nothing about the body you found. What are you looking for?"

Again, it was Kate who answered, "We need to see your personnel files, and those of the girls who were in your care, for the years 2004 through 2005, and I'd like you to take me to them now."

"What's going on?" Billy Dickerson said. His face was red, he was angry and he was flanked by Darius Willett and an even bigger man I knew to be Mickey, the Mouse, Donavan. He was a scary-looking critter, big, heavy, greasy dreads and a beard; he looked like a damned terrorist.

"Lonnie," I said. "These two will both be armed. You might want to take care of that."

"Yeah, we talked about that." He took a step forward, his hand out toward Willett.

"Give!" he said.

Willett looked at Dickerson, who nodded, then reluctantly handed over the .45 Colt M1911.

"Now you," Lonnie said to Donavan.

The man reached behind his back, brought forth a .40 Glock 22, and handed it to Lonnie. Lonnie unloaded the clips from both weapons, cleared the chambers, and emptied the clips, then he placed them on the desk.

"You guys have permits for those?" he asked.

They both nodded, slowly. Willett's eyes were narrow slits, his mouth a thin tight line.

"I need to see 'em, now."

They pulled billfolds from jeans pockets and handed the permits to Lonnie. He checked them carefully, eyes back and forth from face to permit. Finally he nodded and handed them back.

All the while Lonnie was so engaged, I was half listening to the conversation Kate was having with the Dickersons. I missed most of what was said, but tuned in just as India was trying to convince us that no computer records for those years existed, only paper files, and even those were sparse.

I was inclined to believe her. I had an idea that these two were not the most meticulous record keepers, but more than that, I figured the last thing they would do if they were into prostitution would be to keep incriminating records. Still, you never know.

"Tim," I said. "See what you can find."

"May I take a look at your computers, please?" Tim asked India.

"Forget the please," I said. "Just do it."

He grinned and walked around the desk to the keyboard.

"Now, show me the files," Kate said, in a tone of voice that brooked no argument.

"This way," India said, and walked across the big room and through the door next to Billy Dickerson's office. Oh, she was pissed.

The room was sparsely furnished, just a table, a half dozen one-time dining chairs, a credenza, and two tall, steel file cabinets. She was right. There was almost nothing for the transition period in 2005. In fact, there wasn't much for any of the years from then until now. The whole lot was contained in a single drawer.

"There," India said, angrily. "Satisfied?"

"There's almost nothing here," Kate said. "You must have taken in hundreds of people. Why have you not kept proper records?"

She simply shrugged, didn't answer.

"Mrs. Dickerson, I do not believe you have been running this facility for more than ten years and you have not kept records. Now, let's try again. Where are your records?"

"This is it. There are no more. Billy," she said, as she looked at her husband, "isn't the most professional manager... he just didn't bother."

Billy Dickerson said nothing; he just stood and glared at his wife.

"Sergeant Guest." Kate turned to Lonnie. "I want this place taken apart. Tell the uniforms what we're looking for. I also want any computers, including the one Tim is searching. We're looking for desktops, laptops, tablets, and especially external drives and data disks. Seize them all. We'll take them with us."

"Oh my God," India said. "You can't do that. How will we be able to run this place without the computer?"

"I can, and I will. You'll manage. You have so far." Kate turned to me. "Mr. Starke. Do you have anything you want to say?"

"That I do, to both of them. I have some questions. Shall we sit?"

We sat. Kate and I on one side of the table, the Dickersons on the other. Willett and Donavan stood behind them, leaning against the wall. Billy clasped his hands on the table in front of him, his face twisted into a snarl. India did her best to retain her composure, but it was easy to see it was a fight she was already losing: her lips were pursed, eyes

223

narrowed, brow furrowed in a frown. She tapped her fingernails on the tabletop. She was both angry and nervous.

I have always found that the best way to get a reaction to a question is to assume the person or persons being questioned knows the answer.

"Tell me about Brinique Williams, Billy." I watched their eyes: nothing.

"Tell you about who? I don't think I know anybody with that name."

"Yeah, you do. She was one of the waifs and strays you took in back in the day, when you were at Hill House."

I could see that the name Hill House bothered him, but I was still not sure about the girl.

He slowly shook his head, looking puzzled. "It doesn't ring a bell. There were so many. Why do you want to know?"

Her parents were here. They wanted to know what happened to her. I think you took her in. I also think you put her out on the streets. Hell, Billy, you may even have sold her on, you or your pal Sal De Luca."

That got to him.

"*You son of a bitch,*" he yelled, raising himself up on his hands. "What kind of operation d'you think

224

I'm running here? I'm saving these kids, not destroying them."

India grabbed his arm and pulled him down.

"That you are, Billy," I said. "I know exactly what you're doing. You'd better calm down. I wouldn't want you to have a heart attack, especially with so many needy kids relying on you."

He took a breath, looked round at the two heavies, then at me, and nodded.

"I have another question for you, Billy. Tell me what you know about Ricky Jessell." This time I caught it. It wasn't much, but it was there. I can always tell, and he wasn't the only one. Willett's mouth also tightened.

Dickerson thought for a minute, as if he was racking his brains, then he shook his head. "Can't say that I do. I see so many young people during the course of our endeavors; can't remember all of them."

I smiled at him. He tried to hold my gaze, but he couldn't.

"I didn't say he was young, Billy. What makes you think he was?"

"I, I, I," he stuttered. "I just... well... I assumed, you know. All the kids I deal with are young."

I nodded. I did know.

"Where is he, Billy?"

He looked at me, his eyes narrowed, his lips clamped together in a tight line, his face flushed as anger once again pushed its way to the front.

"Screw you, Starke. I told ya, don't know any Ricky Jessell, nor no Brin... whatever her name is. Now get the hell out of here."

There was a knock at the door. It opened and Lonnie pocked his head inside.

"We found something," he said.

Kate beckoned him in. He placed a stack of $100 bills in front of her. She looked up at him, then at the money, touched the stack, and looked at the Dickersons. They showed no reaction.

"More'n $100,000," Lonnie said. "It was in a small safe in one of the back rooms."

"That's a lot of money," Kate said. "Where did you get it?"

"If I remember correctly," India said. "Your warrant states you may only look for files, records, and such. It makes no mention of money. I suggest you put it back where you found it. I do not have to explain it." *Hell, she's right.*

"That's true," Kate said. "Put it back, Sergeant." He did.

I looked at Kate. She said nothing. Her eyes were focused on the two Dickersons. I leaned forward, placed my elbows on the table, clasped my hands together in front of my chin, and stared at Billy. For a moment he held my gaze, then he looked away, shifted in his seat, looked at his wife, then back at me.

"Whaaat?" he asked.

"You know what I think, Rev?" I said. "I think that money is a payoff for services rendered. I think you and De Luca are in bed together. I also think you have quite an operation going here: you find the girls, and boys, and he handles the practical side of things."

"You stinkin' piece of... of... garbage." He was so angry he could barely spit the words out. "You don't know what you're talkin' about. We run a legitimate charitable institution here. We do a lot of good, provide homes, food, and help. That money was from donations. You... you...you." He ran out of air, gulped and was about to begin again when India stopped him.

"Stop it, Billy. Calm down. They have nothing. There's nothing to find. Let 'em have their fun. They'll soon be gone, and we'll still be here."

Hmmm, I wonder. It's all a little too pat. Where are their records? There must be some; more than the little we've found. How can you handle hundreds of people and not know who, when, where, what and how? There has to be records for the money; he said donations.

227

If this is a 501c3, that money has to be accounted for, to the IRS. And she has a funny look on her face, a smirk.

I sat, befuddled. Yes, he was upset, and so had she been, but now, not so much. I had to wonder.

Finally, Kate broke it up. She pushed her chair back; it scraped noisily. She stood, looked down at them both, and said, "This is not yet over." Then she turned and, without waiting for me, walked out of the office door.

"She's right, Billy," I said. "You know something. What, I don't know, but I'll find out. I think a call to the IRS will loosen things up a little." That got him. "Oh, and by the way, it was Brinique Williams we found under the floor." I watched them both as I said it; there was no reaction from either one of them, or from the two clowns leaning against the wall. I decided to throw a little more bait into the pond. This time it was Willett I watched.

"We found another body at Hill House, Billy." It seemed like everyone had stopped breathing, it was so quiet.

"Not interested? Now that is strange. It was a male, about eighteen or nineteen years old. He'd been stuffed into the drain in the basement. We think it was Ricky Jessell." Nobody moved. Billy glowered at me through narrowed eyes. Donavan and Willett were all attitude, defiant, challenging. I smiled, rose to my feet. "Have a nice day, Billy," I said, with a smile. "I know I will."

Outside the office, at the far end of the community room, by the desk, Lonnie, Kate, Tim, and three uniforms were making ready to leave. They had nothing, except a single laptop and the desktop computer, and a few paper files; no drives or disks.

We made our way back down the stairs and along the corridor to the outer door. Again, I wondered about the doors.

"Did anyone get to look inside these rooms?" I asked Lonnie.

"Yep, all of them. They're empty, no lights, couldn't see anything, had to use flashlights. Just some old broken furniture. Must have been living places back in the day."

I nodded. Back in the car, as Kate drove me back to my office, I reran the interview in my head. I had a feeling we'd missed something, that the Dickersons were hiding something, maybe a lot.

"What about the top floor?" I asked.

"There were a dozen bedrooms up there, Lonnie said, all of them occupied. Some had girls, three were for males, I think. Looked clean and tidy. Didn't find anything."

I shook my head. Something was missing. I could feel it. *Damn. If those two aren't as crooked....*

The bastards are trafficking. I know they are, and they're in deep with De Luca. What the hell are we missing? I gotta figure it out!

Chapter 25

When we left Cherry Street, I was in a blue funk. I had them drop me off at my office. Tim went with Kate, Lonnie, and the computers to the PD on Amnicola. He would copy anything he found onto thumb drives and we'd go ever everything together. It was after four o'clock when I banged against the front door. *Wow. It's locked. That's a first.*

I waited until Jacque turned the lock and then I pushed through into the outer office; Jacque was alone, and that upset me; no, it made me damned angry.

"What the hell is going on around here?" I asked. "You're not supposed to be here by yourself; no one is. Where's Bob?"

"Calm down, Mr. Starke." She never could bring herself to call me by my first name, even when we were alone. "I'm fine. The door was locked. I wouldn't have let anyone in I didn't know. Bob was called out. Something to do with his daughter. He said he'd be back."

I nodded; she was right. She was safe enough, short of an all-out attack on the office, which wasn't likely, even though De Luca was one crazy son of a bitch. Bob? He was a law unto himself, could come and go as he pleased. I shook my head and went to my office.

"Hey, Jacque," I yelled through the open door. "You busy?"

"Not so much. What do you need?"

"A cup of coffee. Would you mind?" Now that was something I never did, ask Jacque to wait on me. In fact, this was a first.

"What's wrong?" she asked, as she set the cup down in front of me and then sat down in front of the desk. That was another first. In all the time she'd worked for me, she'd never sat down without being asked.

"I dunno. I feel kinda... I dunno, kinda washed out, I suppose. And this thing with De Luca has me all knotted up, which is exactly what he wanted."

I looked at her. The concern was etched deep on her face. She knew I was never one to worry much about anything. I sat there for a moment, sipping my coffee.

"Harry," she said. *Wow, this is a day for firsts. Now she calls me by my first name.*

I smiled at her, but didn't answer.

"You need some time off," she said. "You need to get away. My folks have a place on the island. They're here for Christmas. They would be pleased to let you have it for a few days. You could relax, chill out, swim, fish, sleep. I'll call them." She started to get up.

232

"Wait. Just like that? It's a bit sudden, don't you think? It's a great idea, but...."

"Give me a minute," she said.

I heard her in the outer office, on the phone, talking, her soft Jamaican accent more pronounced than usual. *She must be talking to her father.*

She hung up the phone, and I heard her rummaging around in her desk drawer.

"Here," she said, placing a set of keys down in front of me. "Those are mine. It's all fixed. All you need do is get there. They won't be going home until after the New Year. The house is yours until then."

"Wow, Jacque. You are something else, but I dunno. Give me a minute alone. Do you mind?"

She smiled, nodded, and closed the door behind her.

I picked up the keys and turned them over between my fingers, thinking. *Damn. It would be nice. Sun, sea and sand, and... Amanda? But first....Well, I have to get there. Too late to book a damn flight.*

I picked up my cell phone and dialed the number. It rang a half dozen times. "You've reached August Starke. Leave a message."

"Hey, Dad. I know you're there. Pick up the damn phone." And he did.

"What's up, son?"

"Are you using the Lear over the holidays?"

"No, not until I leave for New York on the second. Why, do you want to use it?"

"Depends on Joe and Sarah. I want to go to Jamaica, but I've left it a bit tight. Tomorrow is Christmas Eve. We'd need to go this evening if they are to be back tomorrow, in time for their Christmas."

"Give me a couple of minutes. I'll call him. See if we can make it happen. It will cost you: two round trips. Not so much as last year, though. Fuel is down by more than forty percent. I'll call you right back." Click. I looked at the phone, shook my head. *Why does he always do that?*

Less than ten minutes later, he called back. "Harry, the Lear is fueled and ready to go; it always is. Joe says they can go tonight, but he needs to know when. He has to file a flight plan. You have his number. Why don't you give him a call?"

I thanked him and said I would do just that. *Hah, even though he can be an ass sometimes, my old man never fails to come through for me. That's one hell of a perk.*

I called Amanda and told her to pack for a week. Next I called Kate and told her I was leaving for a few days and that I'd be back on the 29th, or whenever Joe was available. I wanted to be home for the New Year. It wasn't an easy call. She wanted to know the ins and outs of a duck's... well, you know.

I told her to work with Tim, if she needed him, while I was gone, and that Bob would be on call, too. I couldn't see her needing Bob, but Tim, for sure.

I had just finished my call to Kate when Bob walked in through the front door; he was followed a minute later by Heather. I sat them down and explained what I was about to do. It always had been my intention to close the office that night, to give everyone Christmas Eve and the following week off, and I saw no reason to change any of that. I did, however, warn everyone to be vigilant and take extra care when out and about. Then I called Tim and told him that under no circumstances was he to spend time in the office alone, and that I would fire him if I found out that he did. *I wouldn't, but he didn't know that.*

Finally, I looked around the office, picked up Jacque's keys, hugged her, and walked out to the lot where the Explorer was parked. It was but a small chance that I happened to look across the street just as a black BMW cruised slowly past the gate. The windows were dark tinted, and I couldn't see who was driving, but I had a good idea. *Goddamnit. Well, can't do anything about it now.*

I went back into the office and made sure Bob would see everyone safely off the premises, and that everything was secured, the alarms turned on, etc.

"For Christ's sake, Harry. Get the hell out of here. Go have a good time. I'll take care of everything. Okay?"

I grinned at him, and did just that. By six-thirty that evening, I was seated beside an excited Amanda, sipping on three fingers of Laphroaig heading east to Montego Bay at 520 miles per hour.

The next seven days went by quickly, too quickly. We had a ball: we scuba dived, swam, sailed, even played nine holes of golf on the White Witch at Rose Hall. I always wanted to do that.

Amanda was amazing. She looked like a goddess, day or night, no matter what we were doing. She was like a kid. She played in the sand, splashed in the shallow, emerald waters of the Caribbean, nibbled her food, drank copious amounts of wine, and, well, you don't want to know the rest. It was the best Christmas I'd had since I was a child.

By Tuesday morning, the 29th, I was getting antsy, and was ready for the flight home. Joe was due into Montego Bay at noon, and we were there waiting for him. I bought him and Sarah, his co-pilot, lunch, and we were in the air and heading west by one-thirty. There was an hour time change, to the good, and we landed at Lovell Field at three-thirty. An hour later, we were safely back at Lakeshore Lane, a fire burning, drinks in hand, and on the sofa enjoying the view.

Good times they had been, but they were behind us, and I already was experiencing forebodings of the nightmare that was surely to come.

Sooner or later, I would have to deal with De Luca face to face.

Chapter 26

The next few days also flew by quickly. I heard from Kate. The case was almost at a standstill. They were still combing through the files, from both organizations, and Kate was awaiting results on any possible DNA match that might throw some light on the identity of the body in the drains.

I called Jacque, made sure all was well with her. It was; the office wasn't due to reopen until January 4. Next, I called her parents and thanked them for the hospitality and the wonderful time we'd enjoyed. I called Bob; all was well there, too. Tim, however, had spent most of his time at the PD, going through the files. What time he did take off, he spent with Sam. *Hah, I knew that was coming. Good for you, Tim.*

Next, I wrote a check to my dad for almost $16,000 to cover the costs of the Lear and Joe and Sarah's time, and I considered it worth every penny. Finally, I settled down again, relaxed, and let Amanda cook lunch. Now when I say cook, what she actually did was make sandwiches.

For the New Year, we went to the club and spent it with my mother and father, and my idiot brother, Henry, who prefers to be called Hank. The more he had to drink, the more Amanda had to fight him off, a task she thoroughly enjoyed. During one quiet moment, I took the old man aside and handed him the check. He looked at it, smiled, and tore it up.

"Happy New Year, son. I envy you."

The rest of the holiday was spent lounging around the condo, eating, drinking, and enjoying what I supposed must, for most folks, be wedded bliss. Hell, I even played golf with the old man; the old devil beat me handily, as always. He took more glee from taking that ten-dollar bill from me.... Damn.

The only dark spots of the entire Christmas-New Year period were the storm clouds brewing in the distance, and I'm not talking about the weather.

Salvatore De Luca was never very far from my thoughts.

Chapter 27

The office was cold when I arrived a little before eight that first Monday morning of 2016. Someone had turned the heat down to sixty-four degrees. I turned it up and almost immediately felt the blast of warm air across my legs. Thank the Lord for gas heat.

One by one, they came dragging in through the side door. First Jacque, then Bob, Tim, and everyone else. I made myself a coffee, black, and went into my office. The files we had taken from the Dickersons still lay there on my desk, unopened. Tim must have put them there sometime during the holiday.

In the outer office, I could hear them, talking together about their experiences. For a moment, I was tempted to join the fun, but it was then that my cell phone buzzed. I looked at the screen. Kate.

"Hey, you," I said. "How the hell are you?"

"Not as good as you, I bet." *Oh, hell.*

It was then I realized it was the first Christmas and New Year I hadn't spent with Kate in more than ten years. I felt like shit.

"Harry? You still there."

"Yeah. Kate. I'm sorry...."

"Oh hell, Harry. Don't even go there. You don't owe me a thing, okay? Now, what are you doing? We need to talk. I'm headed that way. Are you free?"

"Well, yeah, but...."

"Good. See you in ten." Click. *Geeze. Where does she get that from? She never used to do that.*

She was here in eight, and she was as feisty as a terrier on steroids. She stamped into my office, a tall Starbucks cup in her hand. As always, she looked stunning, even dressed as she was for the weather. She was wearing jeans tucked into high-heel boots that came almost up to her knees, a white turtleneck sweater under a heavy, black North Face Denali coat, and a white wool hat. She was carrying a slim briefcase.

She took off the heavy coat, laid it down on one of the chairs, sat down heavily in another, the Glock at her waist slamming against the arm, and stretched out her legs.

"So," she said, with a huge grin on her face. "Look at you. You caught some sun. How was the Caribbean? No, no, no," she held up her hand to stop me answering, "forget it. None of my business. Still, it looks like you had a nice time."

I just looked at her and shrugged. I didn't think she was quite as chipper as she made out.

"I needed it, Kate. I did some serious thinking while I was out there, mostly about De Luca. You do realize that one of us is probably going to die before this is over, don't you?"

"Not if I can help it. This is not the OK Corral, Harry. We don't do High Noon anymore. You have to leave it to the police."

"Hah," I said. "You can't do a thing until he makes a move. Then it will be way too late, and what if, in the meantime, someone gets hurt, or killed? The man is crazy; he's a nut job. He has to be stopped. We're all walking around looking over our shoulders, living behind bars, security systems. That can't go on; not indefinitely."

She nodded. "You're right, but you can't take matters into your own hands. I won't allow it."

She meant it, I could tell, but she wasn't the one with the responsibility for almost a dozen other people. I was, and she could tell by the look on my face that I wasn't having any of it.

I changed the subject. "So what did you need to talk to me about?"

"We have a DNA profile back for the body in the drain, but we don't have a match, at least not yet. There's nothing on the NCIC or CODIS databases. Whoever he was, he's not going to be able to help us. Do you think Sam might like to do another head?"

"Dunno. We can ask her. I'll have to pay her this time though, but don't worry about that. I'll handle it."

She nodded. "We need to sit down, all of us, and try to figure out exactly what we do have."

"We can do that now if you like, before the office winds back up again. Are you done with Tim?"

"I am. He's been very helpful. We now have a working list of people who were lodged at Hill House during the period when the Draycotts took over, and just after. We also have a list of sorts gleaned from what little information was available on the Dickersons' two computers. Were you able to do anything with those files?" she asked, nodding at the pile on my desk.

"Er no. I just got back. I planned to go through them this morning. Can I have copies of the lists?"

"Yes, of course." She dug into the briefcase and brought forth several sheets of paper stapled together.

"They are listed in order by date of residence. Tim has already managed to run some of them down, which was one of the things I wanted to talk to you about. We need to set up interviews, and I'd like for us to do them together, here, if you don't mind. This is much more comfortable for what I have in mind than an interview room on Amnicola."

"Sure. When do you want to start?"

"As soon as possible. Tomorrow, if we can."

I nodded. "Do you have a list with phone numbers?"

"I do." Again she delved inside the case and came up with a single sheet of paper on which were eleven names.

"We can start with these," she said, handing it to me. "I also have the files for each of them out in the car."

I glanced at the names. Nothing jumped out at me, but then why would it.

"I'll have this copied, and the files, if you don't mind, then I'll have Jacque make the calls and see if we can get started. How's that?"

She hesitated for a moment, then said, "I'd rather the calls were made by a sworn officer. It would carry more weight. I took a liberty and brought a female officer with me. She's waiting in the outer office."

"Well, have her come in then. Let's brief her. She can use the back office."

Kate rose to her feet, opened the door, and beckoned. "Officer Susan Beckham, this is Mr. Harry Starke. Harry, Susan."

I rose, leaned over the desk and shook her hand, and then I sat back and listened as Kate gave her instructions. The idea was to persuade them to come to this office starting at nine in the morning, at thirty-minute intervals. Kate would do the interviews and I would sit in. If anything grabbed my attention,

I would chime in. We didn't expect them all to come in, but we needed at least a half dozen, and the request was to be presented firmly and with the authority of the police department backing it up.

When we were done, I had Jacque take her to the back office and show her how the phone system worked. I also had her put a block on the system so it wouldn't show the caller or the number.

"Okay," I said, when Officer Beckham had left. "What else do you have for me?"

"Something that will interest you greatly," she replied. "On Tuesday last week, when you and Amanda were splashing about in the sunshine, we picked up two hookers. Both of them were under age."

She paused and looked at me, smiling. I waited, nothing.

"Well, damn it. What?"

"They both claimed they wanted out...."

"No shit," I said. "Did they implicate anyone? De Luca, Dickerson?"

She shook her head. "No, not yet. They both clammed up, asked for lawyers. One of them is only fifteen; the other is sixteen. They were working the hotels, together, as a team, a twosome. I think there's more, but they weren't talking, either of them. They're young, very scared. We still have them at the

PD. I was thinking that you should talk to them, unofficially. You're not a cop. They just might open up to you."

I nodded. "Let's do it. When?"

She looked at her watch. "It will have to be at the department. I already have Johnston's tentative approval, which is enough for now. It's nine-thirty now. Why don't you meet me there, say in half an hour?"

"I'll be there. I think it might be a good idea for me to see them together. Yeah, I know; that's not how it's done, and that's exactly why I want to do it that way. Have them ready when I get there."

"Nice to have you back, Harry," she said, as she rose to her feet. "Maybe you can buy me lunch sometime."

She turned and walked out of the door without a backward look. I felt like an ass.

Chapter 28

Kate was waiting in the lobby when I arrived at the police department on Amnicola Highway. She ushered me through security, pinned a visitor's badge on me, and walked me through to one of the interview rooms. They were already sitting together at the table, drinking Cokes from cans. *Oh boy, these are a rare couple to be sure.*

Under the cold fluorescent lights, they looked pathetic. Two underweight, under-dressed waifs, one blonde, one redhead; both would have looked more at home in a Dickensian orphanage. *Talk about Oliver Twist.*

They did have coats on, of sorts: those quilted, shiny things. They both wore miniskirts that barely covered their asses, and tight sweaters that showed just how underendowed they both were. Most ludicrous of all were the shoes they were wearing: stiletto heels at least five inches high. Neither one of them carried a purse. I guessed they must keep whatever few belongings they possessed in their coat pockets.

"Hey, girls. How are you?" I asked. "Can I get you anything?"

"I could use a smoke," the blonde one said. "Who the hell are you?"

"My name is Harry Starke. You can call me Harry. I'm a private investigator. I'm here to try and help you, and no, you can't have cigarettes; you're too young."

"They why don't you take a hike, *Harry*? We have nothing to say to you."

I nodded, looked at the plate glass mirror, behind which I knew Kate and several other officers were watching, including the chief, I shouldn't wonder.

"I understand how you feel," I said. "I—"

"Like hell you do." This time it was the redhead who spoke. "Why don't you just leave us alone? They have to let us go soon."

"No, they don't. You were caught offering yourselves for prostitution, at one of those goddamn short-stay, ten-buck an hour, no-tell motels, for God's sake, and you're both under age. That means you get turned over to Children's Services."

"So what," the redhead said. "You think they can hold us? They couldn't before. We'll be outa there before they draw the goddamn drapes."

"Okay," I said. "That's enough. Just hear me out for a minute. I'm trying to help you get yourselves out of this mess. You do want out, don't you?"

They looked at each other, then down at the table. The blonde, the younger of the two, whispered something I couldn't hear. The redhead shook her head, put her hand reassuringly on her friend's arm, looked up at me and said, "So talk. I ain't sayin' anythin', an' I ain't promisin' nothin', but we'll listen."

"Okay, so listen to me. I can get you out of the game and into a nice home, with a proper job, food, clean clothes, warm beds, medical attention, and a chance at a proper life, and I can do it today. You don't have to go back to the life, but you've got to help me to help you. Will you do that?"

"What you talkin' about?" the redhead asked. "What home? Where? We get our own room? Just us two?"

"All in good time. You ready to get out?"

Again, they looked at each other, then at me, and then they both slowly nodded their heads.

"Good, I'm going to ask you some questions, and I'm going to record what you say. I'll get your names, then all you need do, for now, is answer those questions you feel comfortable with. Got that?"

They both nodded.

I opened my iPad. "First, let me get your names." I looked across the table, waiting.

"I'm Terri Stokes. She's Sandra Lutz," the blonde said.

"Terri. You're fifteen, yes?"

"Yes."

"Sandra. You're sixteen?"

"I'll be seventeen in three months," she said truculently.

I smiled at her. "And you're going to live to see your birthday. I promise."

They looked at each other. Terri grabbed the older girl's hand and squeezed it. Then she burst into tears.

It was several minutes before she was able to compose herself enough to continue.

I figured the youngster wasn't about to give up her chance, and that she was the one I needed to concentrate on. I was wrong.

"Terri," I said. "Where are your parents?"

"She ain't got none. They died when she was three. She's bin in fosters ever since, 'till she run away an' I got 'er, that is." Sandra was obviously the alpha of the two.

I nodded. "Okay then. What about you, Sandra? Where are your parents?"

"I ain't got none either, well I 'ave, but they threw me out, well my mom did, when I told 'er about me dad, touchin' me an' all." *Christ! Poor kids. First that, and then this mess.*

"So, Sandra, I need to know; who do you work for?"

She didn't answer.

"You have to answer the question, Sandra."

She shook her head.

"Okay, let's try this: where are you two living now?"

"I cain't tell ya. They'll... they'll... I cain't. You don't need to know all that. All you gotta do is get us out, like you said you would." There were tears running down her face now.

"It's okay, Sandra," I said, gently. I reached across the table and took her hand. It was icy cold. She looked at me, her eyes wide, tears streaming down her face.

"I understand. I really do. You're already out. I'm going to make sure you stay out. Okay?"

She sniffed, nodded, and gazed at me.

"Okay, now I need to know where you *were* living. It's really, really important."

She sniffed again, and said, 'On Cherry Street; we lived in a place on Cherry Street."

My heart almost stopped. I couldn't believe it. She'd just handed us the Dickersons. It was too easy. I had to make sure.

"You mean Blessed are the Homeless? The Reverend Dickerson's shelter?

"Yeah, but it ain't no shelter. He buys an' sells kids, and makes us do stuff, you know, stuff, like at the hotel."

I was stunned, and I know the watchers behind the glass were, too.

"Okay, Sandra. We're doing good. Now think carefully before you answer this next one. Was there anyone else besides the Dickersons involved? Did he send you to see or work for anyone else?" It was a forlorn hope, but what the hell. Who knew who else might be involved in the mess? I had to try.

"I dunno what you mean," she said. "There was him, Mr. Dickerson, 'is wife, 'an two big black guys, an' a couple a others. That's all we saw, weren't it, Terri?"

The youngster nodded.

"The big black guys; what were their names, do you know?"

"Darrel, or somthin'. No, Darius, was one. He called the other one Mouse."

"And you lived in the rooms up on the top floor with the other girls, right? How many were there, other girls?"

252

"Shit. What you smokin'? We lived in the basement; all fifteen of us. There ain't nobody lives up there on the top floor. That's all jus' for show."

I didn't know what to say. I was speechless, dumbfounded.

I shuddered, and I know they heard it when I swallowed. "But those rooms aren't fit to live in," I said. "There are no lights, no heat, nothing."

"What you talkin' about?" Sandra asked. "What rooms? I only seen one room, one big room, with a bathroom, closets, an all. It ain't too bad, just crowded is all. I lived in worse. It's what we have to do for it we don't like."

"Okay, girls. You're going to have to help me out. What big room?"

She screwed up her face. I think she thought I was stupid. "The one at the back, under the kitchen an' stuff."

I drew a rectangle on the legal pad in front of me, pushed the pad across the table to Sandra and said, "That's looking down on the house from above. Draw your room for me, please."

She picked up the pencil and drew a line across the rectangle. There were now two rectangles, one took up two thirds of the floorplan, the other about a third; she put a large cross in the smaller of the two rooms.

253

I looked at it, then at her. "The kitchen and work rooms are above the cross, right?"

She nodded. I took the pencil from her and drew two lines in the bigger rectangle representing the corridor with the empty rooms on either side, then I pushed the pad across the table so they could look at it.

"That, there," I pointed with the pencil, "is a corridor in the basement with rooms on either side."

"Never seen it. Never bin the other side of the wall."

I pulled the pad back and stared down at it. The stairs up skirted the brick dividing wall between the two basement areas. To all intents and purposes, it was a dead end. You'd have to be looking for it to find it, and we weren't, but we should have been. Now I knew what that steel door at the rear was for.

"How did you get in and out of that room, Sandra? Through the steel door at the rear?"

"Ain't no doors at the rear that I know of, it's all smooth concrete." *So that second steel door is a dummy. Hmmm.*

"There's a way down from upstairs," she continued, "but we went in an' out through the front wall of the basement. There's all sorts of tunnels there."

"Okay, girls," I said. "I'm going to need some help with this. Is it all right if I bring in Lieutenant Gazzara and another man?"

They looked at each other, then at me, then Terri said, "But, Mister, you said...."

"I know what I said, and I meant it, and I want you to call me Harry. Okay? Can I bring them in?"

They both nodded, warily. There was a knock at the door. I got up and opened it. Kate and Lonnie came in.

"Kate, this is Terri and Sandra, and girls, the big guy is Sergeant Lonnie Guest. You can trust them both. I promise."

I looked at the two police officers. They were as befuddled as I was. Lonnie leaned over the table, looked at them and said, "Hey, girls. Can I take a peek at this with you?"

The younger one nodded up at him. Sandra just stared up at him.

"Great," he said, and dragged up a chair and set it down beside Sandra. "Now, ladies. If you'll go through it again with me."

I shook my head in amazement. The great bear was trying to make friends with them, and he did. Within minutes, he just about had the two of them eating out of his hands. Hell, they were giggling at him.

255

Kate and I sat at the table facing Lonnie and the girls.

"Tell us about Reverend Dickerson," I said. "How did you get there, with them?"

"The guy, Darius," Sandra said. "He found me first. About a year ago, I s'pose. I got off the bus on Airport Road. He was outside, sat in a nice car, BMW. He was dressed nice. Asked me where I was going. I didn't know. I was fourteen. I... I... just wanted to go somewhere, anywhere. He asked if I was hungry. I was. He bought me a burger. We ate it in the car. We talked. He was nice. He asked if I had somewhere to stay. I didn't. He said he knew a nice place where I could stay 'till I got on my feet. That was it."

She paused, shuddered, then looked sideways, up at Lonnie, and said, "That night, Mr. Dickerson, he screwed me. It was my first time. It hurt so bad." The tears were streaming down her face again.

Lonnie was so angry I thought he was going to blow it, but he didn't. He just gently rubbed the girl's back, shaking his head. At that moment, I knew I would not have wanted to be Billy Dickerson.

Terri's story was almost identical, only she had hitched into town with a truck driver. He dropped her off at the junction of Highway 153 and Shallowford Road. It was just her bad luck that she hitched another ride with... yeah, you guessed it: Darius Willett. She also suffered through the Dickerson initiation, and then Sandra kind of took her under her wing. Fat lot of good it did. All they could offer each other was company, sympathy and a little comfort. From that point on, their every move was strictly controlled.

They were worked every night, seven nights a week; sold, on the streets or in sleazy motel rooms. They even went to private homes, and they were paid nothing. They were housed, clothed, and fed, and that was it.

Lunchtime came and went, and the girls continued to talk, and we continued to record everything they said. By the time it was over, at a little after one-thirty, we had it all; the whole pitiful story.

"What are we going to do with them?" Kate asked, as we looked through the back side of the mirror. "We can't turn them over to Children's Services, not now; not after what they've been through."

"I was thinking the Draycotts," I said, "but right now, that's not an option. Not until we know who murdered the girl and the kid in the sewer."

I leaned against the wall beside the glass, and stared in at the two kids. *Jesus H. Christ. What a goddamn mess. What are we going to do with you?*

I closed my eyes, leaned my head back against the wall....

"Hey, Harry. Wake up," Kate said, shaking my arm.

"I wasn't asleep. I was trying to figure out what to do with them. They need clothes, something to eat, somewhere to stay until we figure out the Draycott thing."

"Hell, Harry. Take 'em home with you." I knew she was joking, but it was something I'd already been considering.

I looked at her, rolled my eyes, and took out my iPhone. I dialed the number and waited.

"Hey, Harry. What's up?"

"Hi, Amanda." Now it was Kate's turn to roll her eyes. She did, and then turned and walked away.

"Listen," I said. "I have a bit of a problem, well, a big problem. I need your help, if you can."

I told her my idea. She was cautiously optimistic. Said she would try, and that I should pick her up at the station; she'd get someone to cover for her. I then went looking for Kate. I found her with Chief Johnston. Neither one of them looked happy.

"So what's the plan?" she asked.

"I need you to release them into my custody."

I thought the chief was going to explode. "Are you out of your gourd, Starke? Those two are hookers, for Christ's sake. We got 'em red handed. Two for one, is what they were selling. We can't let 'em go just like that."

"Okay," I said. "First, they're not hookers; they're victims. Second, they need a goddamn break, and third, I made them a promise, and I intend to keep it. They gave us the Dickersons. All you have to do is tear that place apart. You find that room and the rest of the kids and it's open and shut. No damned misdemeanor this time, no matter who he knows. I'm taking them home with me. Amanda will look after them for a couple of days, while we clear up this Hill House thing, and then, if all goes well, I'll pressure the Draycotts into taking them. That's just an idea, but it's all we have. You send them to DCS and they'll run."

"Okay, okay. Take a breath, Harry. I'll have the papers drawn up. You'll be responsible for them until... well... until we can figure out something else. In the meantime, we're putting together a team to take out the Dickersons. You want in? You deserve it."

259

I said I did, and the time for the raid was set for six o'clock that evening, before the kids were put out on the streets, we hoped. In the meantime, I had work to do.

Chapter 29

"Come on, girls," I said. "Let's get out of here."

"Where?" Sandra asked. "Where you takin' us?"

"I'm taking you home with me."

"The hell you are. You just like all the rest. It ain't gonna be. *Help!*" she yelled at the top of her voice.

I looked at her, my mouth hanging open.

Kate came in, laughing. I knew she'd seen it through the glass.

"It's okay, girls. Harry's one of the good guys. You can trust him. He's taking you to his place on the river to stay with him and his girlfriend for a few days, until we can sort out something permanent. Just be good. He'll treat you right."

I settled the girls into the back seat of the Explorer and headed over to Channel 7. Amanda was waiting in the lobby. I didn't leave the kids in the car. It wasn't that I didn't trust them... you're right, I didn't. So I took them in with me.

I don't think I'll ever forget the sight of Amanda when she spotted them. She stared at them, and then at me. I'm not kidding, her mouth was wide open, her eyes the biggest I've ever seen them. She was dumbfounded. I grinned at her, looked round at the two waifs, and saw why. They were snuggled up together, arm in arm, and they looked like two skinny, teenage Barbie Dolls in short, quilted coats, miniskirts, tight sweaters, and five-inch heels. If they hadn't looked so pathetic, I swear it would have been hilarious. As it was, they were more than a little impressed themselves. The look on their faces when they saw Amanda was a sight to behold.

"Is she real?" I heard Terri whisper, to Sandra.

"Yeah," I said, with a smile. "She's real, and she's really nice. Amanda, come and meet Terri and Sandra."

To this day, I have no idea what was going through Amanda's mind when she greeted those two kids, but she did it.

Now you have to know something about Amanda. This was a very big deal. She's an only child. Never in her life had she been around kids. This was a first, and I was impressed. Not that I'm an expert. I haven't been around that many myself.

""Okay," I said, when we were all back in the car. "This is how it's going to be. Amanda is going to drop me off at the police department, then she's going to take you home and get you both cleaned up, and give you something to eat. Aincha, Momma?"

I thought Amanda was going to choke.

"Then," I continued, "she's going to take you shopping, buy you some decent clothes. You'll stay

262

with us for a few days, no more than that, until I can sort out something permanent."

"You said you already had a place for us; was you lyin' to us?" Sandra asked.

"Nope. I do have somewhere, but I have a couple of issues to sort out first. Okay?"

I looked at her in the rearview mirror; she nodded.

I pulled up outside the PD and got out. Amanda also got out and came around the front to get into the driver's side.

"Here," I said, as she fastened her seatbelt. I handed her my American Express card. "Get them what they need, everything, and look after them. Don't let them out of your sight; they're very fragile."

"Hey, Amanda." Kate waved at her from the entrance to the PD. "Good luck." I'm not sure if she was being facetious or if she meant it. Whatever, Amanda thought she did, and waved back at her as she drove out of the lot. Me? Hell, I fervently hoped I was doing the right thing. I watched them go, shook my head, and followed Kate into the building.

"Kate, was Tim able to find anything on the Dickersons' computers?"

"I don't know. Why don't we ask him? He's in the computer lab."

"Hey, Buddy," I said.

He was seated in front of the laptop, and looked about ready to quit for the day. "Oh, hey, Harry. I was just about to call you. Here." He handed me a thumb drive, and another to Kate. "There's an Excel file on there. It was encrypted, and they'd tried to bury it, but they didn't know how to do it, amateurs. If they'd been savvy, it wouldn't have been on the computer at all, but, hey, it was pretty easy to find and decode. It looks like they were advertising the girls on the web. Classifieds, but I haven't been able to run down the exact sites yet. They were selling them out of Cherry Street, taking calls: hotel visits, home visits, quickies in cars, you name it, and for anything and everything from role-playing to BDSM. Lots of nasty stuff. Oh, and it looks like they were paying off De Luca. That would be his connection to the Dickersons; he was taking a cut, a big one."

He hit a couple of keys on the laptop and the file opened. It didn't mean anything to me, not right then. I would need some time with it.

"It has a kind of spreadsheet on it ordered by month going back to 2013," Tim continued. "Girls' names, places, times, money, and so on. It also has the names of what I presume to be the johns. There are hundreds of them, and that info includes credit card numbers, phone numbers, social security numbers, birthdates, even addresses in some cases. Someone has done a lot of background checking into those folks. I'm thinking possible identity theft. The meta data shows India Dickerson is the author of the file, and that she was the last one to update it."

I looked at Kate. She was smiling.

"Do we have enough there to hang them, Tim?" I asked.

"It's a good start. Put it together with a couple of witnesses and... yep. I think you do. Harry, I'm beat. I need to eat and I need to sleep. Tomorrow?"

"Yes, go on, get out of here. Good work, Tim. I love you, man. Oh, wait, before you go. Do you think Samantha could do another head for us? I'll pay her this time."

"I'm sure she will. Do you have the skull?"

"Carol is making one for us. Give her a call. If it's ready, go get it. Okay?"

"Yep. I'll let you know what Sam says."

"So. Are you ready to go?" Kate asked, when we got back to her office.

"As always," I replied.

She took the Glock from its holster, checked the load, grabbed her coat, and said, "Then let's go join the crew."

And quite a crew it was. She and Lonnie would head the squad, which included a SWAT team of ten, five cruisers, and a dozen other officers. The Dickersons were in for quite a surprise.

Chapter 30

By six-fifteen that evening, we had the building on Cherry Street surrounded. It was already dark, but Kate and I were parked out front and we could see the big old house by the light of the street lamps. It was then I noticed, for the first time, the arched tops of four windows, two on either side of the front door. Only the topmost eighteen inches were visible; the bulk of the windows were below the pavement. I realized then that this was not a two-story building at all; it was, or had been, actually three stories. What once had been the ground floor was now the basement, the doors to which, well one of them at least, opened up onto the original street level of the late 1800s.

Then I realized what I was looking at. It was something I'd heard about in high school and hadn't thought of since. This was part of Underground Chattanooga.

Underground Chattanooga is an abandoned level of the city, the old street level of the late 19th Century, all of it now underground and long forgotten, remembered only in legend and ghost stories. There was a time when Chattanooga was a busy trading post on the river, just a few feet above

267

water level. In 1867, the water rose almost sixty feet above its normal level and flooded the entire city. Chattanooga was growing, so something had to be done. The answer was to raise the street level. Chestnut, Broad, Market, and Cherry, from the river to Martin Luther King Boulevard, then 9th Street, were raised from between four to fifteen feet, depending on their original elevation. The buildings, however, were not raised; ground floors became basements or were abandoned, and that was what we were looking at now.

That lower corridor that led to the stairs was once the ground floor, and so was that hidden area we now knew was beyond the stairs.

The only way through that steel basement door was either to blow it, or for it to be opened from the inside. That being so, Kate decided to take a more direct approach, one that would not give the Dickersons an opportunity to clear the building, as they obviously had on our previous visits. I agreed with her. We would go in through the front door on Cherry Street.

"I get the impression that the front door is never used," I said. "There's a padlock and chain on the outside, but I didn't notice if it was barred on the inside."

"No matter," she replied, staring at the door. "The SWAT boys will have no trouble busting it down."

She got on the radio and began issuing instructions. The plan was that SWAT would go in through the front, followed by Kate, Lonnie, me, and six officers. One of those officers would head straight for the stairs and open the basement door for more officers. The other five would secure the ground floor, including the kitchen area and service rooms. If all went well, it would be over and done with in less than thirty minutes.

I thought she was being a little optimistic, but who the hell am I?

We exited the vehicles, and SWAT ran for the front door. Amid a great deal of yelling and shouting, the door was breached. More than a dozen officers, followed by our small party, charged through the opening and spread out across the first floor, weapons drawn, some heading for the area behind the desk, the offices at the rear of the communal room. The designated officer ran on, down the stairs. Two minutes later, a dozen more uniforms charged up the stairs, and for a few minutes, chaos reigned.

India had backed up against the wall behind the desk, her hands high. Lonnie grabbed Billy Dickerson and slammed him face up against the wall

269

beside her, cuffed him, then grabbed him by the scruff of his neck and dragged him out into the center of the room, his feet barely touching the floor. I thought Lonnie was going to hammer him with his weapon, but somehow he managed to get ahold of himself.

"You piece of shit," he growled in Dickerson's ear. "Just move a goddamn inch and I'll smash your sick, stupid face to pulp."

Mouse Donavan was face down on the floor, cuffed, with his hands behind his back. Of Willett, there was no sign.

Billy's face was white. I don't know if it was from fear, shock or anger; he certainly was angry. India was in an almost trance-like state. She still had her arms stretched, full reach, above her. Kate reached up, grabbed her wrist, and pulled her out from behind the desk, to stand beside her husband. They were a forlorn-looking pair.

"Get this sick son of a bitch away from me," Billy mumbled. "I want my lawyer. I'll have your goddamn jobs."

"So, Reverend Dickerson," Kate said, holstering her weapon, and looking around the crowded room, "you can call your lawyer when we get you back to the station, but first, where are they?"

"Where are who?"

270

"Let's not screw around, Billy. You know who. The girls... and boys, I guess. They certainly aren't in here, and there's no one up on the top floor either."

"I don't know what you're talking about."

"Bull," Kate shouted. "Where the hell are they?" She turned to me, the question unspoken.

I nodded, turned to Lonnie, and said, "Let's go." We ran past the desk into the kitchen area, nothing. *Where the hell is Willett?*

It didn't take more than a couple of minutes before we found it, at the back of what I assumed to be the pantry. A heavy wooden door that looked older than the building itself stood wide open. Someone must have been in a hurry. I went down the steps at the run, the MP9 held out ahead of me. Lonnie was just two steps behind me.

At the bottom of the stairs was a huge open area, a living space, a dormitory with sixteen beds in two rows of eight, but no kids, and worse, no Willett.

"There," I said, pointing. "Sandra said there was a way out. It has to be in that wall."

It was in the corner, difficult to see in the half-light and shadows, another heavy wooden door, and it was locked, from the outside.

"Here, let me," Lonnie said, holstering his weapon. He took two steps back, and then threw himself forward, all 265 pounds of him. His shoulder hit the door. I heard it crack. He hit it again. It cracked more. He backed off at least a dozen feet, took a huge breath, and then hurled himself at the door. This time there was no holding him. The door burst outward and Lonnie hurtled through, landed on the floor, on his face, and lay there, unmoving.

I rushed to his side, grabbed his arm, and pulled. "Hey, Lonnie. You okay?"

He groaned, stirred, rolled over, looked up at me and grinned. Blood was streaming down his face from a deep cut over his left eye.

"Go get 'em, Starke. I'm okay."

I nodded, looked ahead. A string of incandescent bulbs stretched away into the distance, but struggled to breach the darkness. The roof was low, no more than six feet. Rubble, rocks, bricks, great chunks of concrete, and filthy wet sand lay everywhere. Brick-built pillars and round steel supports spaced every few yards held up the roof which must have been Cherry Street. A flight of open wooden stairs led to... nowhere. It was a dank, nightmare world of shadows, rats, and stagnant water, and ahead I could hear someone crying.

I started toward the sound.

"Wait. Hold on. I'm coming with you," Kate shouted, picking her way over the debris.

We didn't have to go far; we couldn't. There was no clear route through the underground city. It was a maze of openings, broken walls, piles of rubble, dead ends, and then we saw light ahead, a square opening to the outside world. I went through first, straight into the arms of a waiting uniformed officer.

"Who the hell are you?" he roared in my ear.

"He's with me," Kate yelled as she breached the opening.

"Oh, sorry, Lieutenant. I thought he was with them." He pointed.

There they were, a forlorn-looking bunch of youngsters, none of them more than sixteen or seventeen years old, a couple no more than eleven or twelve, and... Darius Willett. The officers had him up against the wall, cuffed and waiting for us.

"We were watching the raid going on down there," the sergeant pointed to the now one-time Blessed are the Homeless building some fifty yards away, "and here he comes, bustin' outa the hole in the wall followed by this bunch of kids. There's thirteen of 'em, an' not one of 'em wearin' a coat."

From that point on, there was little left to do other than wrap it all up and haul them all away. DCS arrived with a commandeered church bus and took away the kids.

The Dickersons and their "assistants" were hauled away to the PD where they all lawyered up. There would be no interviews that night, or even the next morning. It wasn't until late the following afternoon that they finally agreed to talk, but only if they could make a deal, and they did. What it was, I had no idea, but talk they did. Implicate Salvatore De Luca, they did not.

It was no more than we had expected. The Dickersons, along with Willett and Donavan, and several others we had yet to apprehend, had been running a sex for sale racket that implicated a lot of well-known members of the public.

Sex with a minor under twelve years of age is rape, a Class A felony in Tennessee; under sixteen, it's a Class B, and there are a whole lot more charges that can be brought for trafficking. The Dickersons were into that in a big way, not to mention that Billy was sampling the product for himself. He was going down, and so were India, Willett, Donavan and the others.... but not, at least for now, Sal De Luca.

Chapter 31

I was in the office by eight-thirty the following morning. Kate arrived a few minutes later and we set up the conference room for interviews: camera, recorder, files, and note pads.

Of the eleven names on the list that Tim had found, Officer Beckham had managed to reach only seven. All of them agreed to be interviewed; the first would arrive at nine o'clock.

Jenny Hollis had been nineteen at the time of the transition of control of Hill House from Dickerson to Draycott. Now, she was almost thirty, married, and had two small children. She was nervous, and when she saw the camera, I thought she was going to walk right back out again. She didn't, and Kate did her best to put her at her ease.

The interview was short. She was at Hill House for only six months, none of them during the Dickersons' reign. I showed her the group photos and asked if she was featured in them. She wasn't. They were taken a couple of days before she arrived. Did she recognize any of the other group members? Yes, several, but she could not remember any names. No, she didn't remember any Brinique. We thanked her for her time, and she left. The second interview was a bust, too.

Number three on the list, Rhonda James, was only fifteen when she arrived at Hill House, and she remembered just about every minute of what she called the worst time of her life. Unfortunately, for us, it didn't last for long. She came to the house with the Draycotts and thus had no knowledge of times or people prior to her arrival in late June of 2005. She did, however, remember the Dickersons, an older boy whose name she never knew, and two of the other girls, one of whom was Jenny Hollis; they were still friends.

Rhonda had been a runaway, and she got lucky. One of the Draycotts' volunteers had found her wandering around the Aquarium after dark; a bad place and time for a young kid to be alone. Her parents came and took her home two weeks after her arrival at Hill House. She was now working as a registered nurse at Erlanger Hospital. *Good for you, girl.*

She looked at the group photos, but remembered none of them, except for herself, a miserable-looking little thing in the front row on the upper balcony.

And so it went on. By one o'clock we had seen them all, and we were no further ahead. Oh, several of them had recognized people in the images; we even managed to gather a few new names, but that was about it. No one remembered Brinique.

I ordered pizzas delivered for the staff and Kate and I retired to my office to eat.

"The girl was there," I said. "She had to have been; she died there, for Christ's sake, but nobody remembers her? That's crazy."

"So what now?" she asked, through a mouthful of cheese and peperoni. *That girl loves her groceries, that's for sure.*

"I don't know. I just don't know. We know she left home on May 27, 2005, and that she was still alive a week later on June 4, because she called her parents. After that, nothing. Not a goddamn thing. I don't think it was the Dickersons."

"Why not?" she mumbled.

"Hell, I don't know that either. It could have been, I suppose. I just had the feeling Billy was telling the truth when he said he didn't know her. That's it. That's all I have."

"That leaves the Draycotts then," she said, "and I don't see that at all."

"Maybe you're right, but I like them for it better than I do Billy."

"So, I'll ask again. What now?"

277

"Same answer. I dunno, and I'm outa here. I need to go see how Amanda's getting on with the kids. I'll call you later, if I think of anything."

I got up from the easy chair, my mind churning. Without thinking, I leaned down and kissed her on the cheek. She almost choked with surprise. Why I did it, I have no idea. Must have been an instinct left over from long ago. Our personal relationship had ended months ago.

"Oh shit. I'm sorry, Kate. I don't know what I was thinking."

"Me neither... oh hell, Harry. It's no big deal. We have a long history together. Forget it."

I said I would, but I was kind of confused, and it started me thinking, but not about anything I'd seriously entertain.... *Hell, who am I kidding? I miss her, goddamnit.*

Chapter 32

Now I have to tell you, I have never been one to think much about domestic bliss. I was forty-two years old, and a confirmed and happy bachelor. I had no intention of ever getting married. I'd seen what that unhappy institution had done to my friends. *How can they live like that? I don't know a single one who isn't miserable, at least now and then.*

So maybe you can imagine what it was like that afternoon when I walked into my living room to find it full of women and kids. *Well, one woman and two kids.*

Yes, I know. I volunteered for it. No matter, it was damned unnerving and it conjured up visions of a future I wasn't sure I wanted, much less could handle. Okay, so dinner was almost ready, and the kids were nicely dressed in new pajamas and were watching television, and Amanda was wearing a cute little apron over.... *Oh my God. It's June Cleaver.*

She stopped what she was doing, came around the breakfast bar, gave me a peck on the lips, said, "Hi, sweetie," and then went back to the stove. I didn't answer. I couldn't. I shuddered, went to the drinks cabinet, and grabbed the first thing that came to hand. I poured a stiff one and sucked it down; ugh. *Damn. I hate neat gin.*

279

Ah, it really wasn't that bad, at least when I remembered that it was only temporary. The kids would soon be gone, and so would Amanda.... *Hmmm.*

We ate dinner. The talk at the table was awkward, stilted, and, well, awkward. We didn't know what to say to one another. For sure, we couldn't talk about the situation the kids had just gotten out of, or the future they would soon have to face.

Fortunately, they both were very tired, and being in the tranquil atmosphere that was my home, even be it essentially a bachelor pad, they soon relaxed and fell asleep on the couch. We got them into bed in the spare room, and damned if we didn't stand in the doorway, Amanda's arm through mine, looking fondly in at them. *Oh no. This is not happening.*

I pulled my arm away, maybe a little too roughly, and it earned me a rather testy look. I grinned at her, took her hand, and led her back to the sofa. I poured her a glass of wine, freshened my Laphroaig, and we settled down for the evening.

The call came at eight-thirty. It was Lucy Haskins, Jacque's long-time partner. She was in a hell of a state, and by the time the call was done, so was I. Jacque had been involved in a hit-and-run accident and was in the hospital, in the intensive care unit.

I explained to Amanda that she had to stay with the kids and I left. This was one of those times when I missed the flashing blue lights and the siren. No, I wasn't legally fit to drive, but I wasn't drunk, and I had no damn choice. On the way across the Thrasher, I called Kate and told her what had happened. She was waiting for me when I screeched into the parking lot at Erlanger Hospital.

Lucy was at Jacque's bedside, holding her hand. She was crying. When she saw us, she jumped up and threw her arms around me. I held her for a moment, then pushed her gently away and looked into her eyes.

"How is she? Have they told you anything yet?" I asked, gently.

"She was hit from the back. She has a broken leg, pelvis, and four broken ribs. They don't know what internal injuries. She also slammed the back of her head on the truck, and look at her poor face." The tears were flowing freely.

Jacque's face *was* a mess. She must have landed face down on the pavement; road rash. Her left cheek and ear were skinned, raw, but it looked superficial. I didn't think it would scar, if she survived. She was unconscious.

"Can you tell me what happened, Lucy?"

"We... we'd been shopping, at the Hamilton Place Mall. We were coming out of Penny's when this truck appeared from nowhere, its engine roaring, like... like it was on a racetrack. It wasn't an accident. He meant to do it. He didn't even slow down. He hit her and screeched off at full speed."

I glanced at Kate; she was recording.

"He must have been doing fifty when he hit her. She... she... she didn't have a chance. Ohhh, Harry. Please tell me she's going to be all right."

I did. I told her. I sat her back down, leaned over and kissed Jacquie on the forehead; nothing, no reaction. *Goddamn it. De Luca! Had to be. You're dead, you son of a bitch; dead!*

"Stay with her, Lucy. I'll go see if I can find a doctor who knows what's going on."

Lucy nodded and took Jacque's hand in both of hers.

"Kate, you'd better come with me. I may need your badge."

I found the doctor who was treating her, but it was a waste of time. He could tell us no more than Lucy had. Oh, she would survive, of that he was quite sure, but what he was worried most about was the bang on the back of the head. There was a hairline crack in the skull and only time would tell if she'd suffered brain damage.

So, I went back to Lucy, and even though no one knew for sure, I told her that Jacque was going to be okay. Kate and I stayed only a few minutes more, and then we left them alone together.

I was in an icy state of calm. To this day, I have no real idea of what my emotions were that night.

I told Kate goodnight, that I would call her the next day, and I left the hospital and drove home, my head full of dark and evil thoughts. At one point, I stopped the car. I was about to make a U-turn and head for De Luca's place, when the reality of what I was thinking set in; now was not the time.

Chapter 33

The phone rang at five-thirty the next morning. I thought the world was ending. I'd forgotten to turn it to vibrate. It was Lucy.

She was excited. Jacque was awake and talking. I got dressed, left Amanda snoring gently, and headed to the hospital.

Jacque's parents were there, in the small waiting room next to the critical care unit. Her mother hugged me, tears streaming down her face. Her father was in a state of shock. He just sat there, staring at the wall, slowly shaking his head.

"Hey," I said. "She's awake. She's going to be fine."

I crept into her room. She smiled up at me, a little ruefully. "I suppose I should take more care and look where I'm goin'." The Jamaican accent was now very pronounced. "Harry, there are some t'ings you need to do...."

"Whoa. You stop right there, young lady. I don't want to hear any more of that crap. Do you hear?"

She nodded and winced. Even that tiny movement hurt her. I was boiling, but so glad to see and talk to her.

"Can you tell me what happened?" I asked.

"Not really. I was crossing the road outside Penny's when I heard this engine roaring. I started to turn to see what it was. I saw this huge truck, well, just the front of it, it was so close, and then.... I woke here."

"Well, it looks like you'll be here for a while, until they fix your leg... and everything. You need to rest, forget about work. We'll manage."

"But, Harry, there's so much to do."

"Nothing we can't handle. I'll have Margo and Leslie take it on until you come back. Lucy." I looked at her, tried to look stern. I'm not sure if it came off. "It's on you. You need to keep her mind off things."

"Hah. You know Jacque. As if anyone could." She was right, of course.

"Well, just do your best. By the way, what color was the truck?"

"It was dark red, old, muddy, with those big wheels. You know; off road, like."

I did know, but I didn't remember ever seeing such a truck, at least not during the past several weeks. Not that I would have taken notice if I had.

The nurse came in. I gave Jacque a peck on the forehead, hugged Lucy, and left them to it, promising to drop in later.

I'm not sure where my mind was when I got back to my car that morning. What with the kids at home, the Dickerson thing, Brinique, and not least what had happened to Jacque. That was no accident. Someone had tried to kill her, and that someone was, I was certain, Salvatore De Luca. I was also certain that he would do it again, unless he was stopped.

It was just after eight o'clock when I arrived at my office. I had to unlock the place myself, something I rarely had to do. Jacque almost always was there before me. The place seemed strangely vacant without her. I made coffee and checked the office voice mail, something else I'd not done for a long time.

The two girls arrived at eight-thirty. They were devastated to hear about Jacque. I gave them their instructions and turned them loose. Bob arrived next with Tim and Ronnie in tow. Heather arrived last. By 8:45 they all knew what had happened, and then I went to my office and closed the door. I needed to be alone,

For almost an hour, I sat at my desk, staring into space, doodling, talking to myself, my mind was in a whirl: odd thoughts, threats, promises, visions, anger, despair, all of those, and more, none of it good.

In my imagination, I saw over and over, Jacquie in front of the truck, its engine howling, tires squealing, the horrified look on her face, her cartwheeling through the air, the back of her head bouncing off the hood, the truck racing away out of the parking lot and out onto Gunbarrel Road. Maybe my imagination was making a bigger deal of it than it actually was, but I didn't think so. I'd seen the results, and the looks on her parents' faces, and I could only sit there, hoping that she would fully recover.

The longer I sat there, the angrier I became. I knew who it was. I also knew I had to put a stop to it before someone else got hurt, or killed. The bastard was turning the screw. He had no intention of getting me, at least not yet. He knew he could hurt me the most by hurting those around me. *Christ. Who the hell will it be next?*

The answer came instantly: no one. He would hurt no one else, because I wasn't going to let him. It had to be him or me.

For another hour, I sat there, mulling it over. It was almost ten o'clock before I thought I might have it. I got up from my desk and walked to the door. All was quiet in the outer office, all except the slow pecking of keys. Bob was writing a report.

"Hey, Bob. Can you leave that until later? We need to talk."

"Sure, just give me a minute to finish this sentence and I'll be with you."

287

I went and sat down in one of the big easy chairs and waited. A couple of minutes later, he joined me.

"What's up, Harry? You look pretty rough."

"Bob, we have to put a stop to this De Luca crap. What if Jacquie doesn't fully recover, ends up crippled, or something? It will be my fault because I didn't stop it sooner. What he did to her was retaliation to what we did to Dickerson. We have to do it before he can hurt anyone else. It's me he's after, but right now he's playing mind games, getting at me through the people I care about. So...."

He stared at me across the table. His eyes half closed. It was a look I knew well, one that boded no one any good. "How far are you willing to go, Harry?"

I looked at him and slowly shook my head. "We can't do it, Bob. We can't just kill him."

"You know as well as I do that to stop it, we have to cut off the head of the snake. We have to kill De Luca. You think he's gonna make a mistake? It ain't going to happen. He's a pro, and he's been doing what he does a long time."

I shook my head, stared at him across the desk. He was right, but how the hell to do it and not go to jail for the rest of my days? That was something I needed to think about. How the hell could we even get at him? He never sets foot outside that restaurant. He even sleeps there; has an apartment above.

"Leave it with me, Bob. I'll give it some more thought."

He rose and turned to leave. "Just don't leave it too long. Somebody in this office dies, it really will be on you."

"Screw you, Bob. That was uncalled for."

He nodded. "Maybe it was, but you know I'm right." He left, closing the door behind him.

I sat there, stewing. What Bob had said hurt, but I knew he was right. I had to take it to De Luca, but how?

I thought about Jacque lying in the hospital. I thought about the two girls who worked in the outer office, Leslie and Margo. Even knowing what had happened to her, they still had turned up for work and were doing their jobs. Bob was right, if anything happened to anyone else, it would be on my head.

Okay, so it's me he wants. He gets his hands on me, I'm dead. Hmmm... he gets his hands on me.... I wonder.... Already, the kernel of a plan was beginning to form. *Could work. If not.... It would mean....*

I picked up the phone and punched the button that would connect me to Bob's extension.

"Hey. What's up?"

"Come on back in here. I have an idea."

For the next hour, Bob and I mulled over my idea. From the start, he could tell I wasn't happy about it, not confident. But Bob is Bob. He went along with it, with reservations.

"Harry, this could bite you in the ass, big time. It goes wrong, you just might not walk away. You do know that, right?"

I nodded. "I do, but I can't think of any other way. He has to be stopped. Either way this goes, it will do that: he'll either be dead or he will kill me. If he kills me, he goes down for that, and it's over."

"If you're sure...."

"I'm not, but it's all we have."

"Then let's do it."

We went over the details several times more, then we both headed out. Tomorrow, as Scarlet said, is another day. I just hoped it wouldn't be my last.

Chapter 34

I was alone when I arrived outside Il Sapore Roma at a little after ten-thirty the following morning. The restaurant wouldn't open for lunch for another hour. I sat there in my car for several moments. I knew I was about to step into the lion's den, and I also knew I had little choice. Was I worried? You bet I was. I was about to face three of the underworld's worst, and alone. *I must be goddam crazy. This works out, I'm done. I'll quit, get me a job selling insurance.... Nah!*

I took a deep breath, checked the M&P9 under my coat, and adjusted the watch on my left wrist. I hoped I wasn't putting too much faith in that thing. *One more time, old buddy; just one more time.*

I got out of the car, locked it, and stood for a moment, looking at the door into the restaurant. I took a deep breath, stepped forward, pushed open the door, and walked through it.

It was dark inside, really dark. The place didn't have windows, and the only the lights on were those above the bar. As always, De Luca was hunched over the bar top with a cup of what I assumed to be coffee. Tony and Jesus were seated together a few feet further away along the bar. He must have heard the door open, because he turned his head and looked at me.

"Well, well. Look who's here. I've been expecting you. Come on and join us, Harry," he said.

He sat there, his elbows on the bar, grinning at me. He looked like a goddamn barracuda.

"You don't seem upset to see me, Sal."

"Oh, Harry. On the contrary. I was hoping you'd drop by. In fact, I was sure you would. I'm very pleased to see you."

"You shouldn't be. I told you what would happen if you touched any of my people. Jacque, my PA, is in the hospital, and one of your thugs put her there. You stepped over the line, Sal."

"That so? Well, wadda ya know?" He looked past me, over my shoulder. "Paulie."

I felt something cold touch the back of my neck. *What the hell?*

"Paulie?" I said. "I don't think I've met you."

"You haven't, Harry. Paulie is my brother. Say hello to Harry Starke, Paulie."

He didn't. The gun didn't move.

"Get your hands up, Starke," De Luca growled. "Tony. Get his gun; frisk him. He might be wired."

I raised my arms, level with my shoulders, the watch angled toward him. He was still hunched over the cup, his mouth twisted into a snarl. He watched

292

as Tony relieved me first of the M&P9 and then patted me down. That done, he nodded at De Luca.

"Don't move a muscle, Starke," De Luca said, sliding off the stool. "Paulie will kill you if you do. It's time to pay your debts, plus a little vig, I think. You know how it works, right? I always need a little vig. Don't go anywhere now, you heah?"

He pushed through the door into the kitchen and returned a minute later, holding a meat cleaver.

"You took my little finger, Starke. I'm gonna take yours, plus interest. I'm gonna take your whole goddam hand. Grab him, Jesus, Tony. Hold his hand on the counter."

Jesus grabbed my left arm and slammed my hand down. Tony grabbed my right wrist and held it like it was in a vice. Paulie still had the gun at my neck. I tried to pull back, but the pressure of the gun against my neck increased. It's funny how weird thoughts flood your mind in times of stress, danger, whatever. *Gotcha, you bastard.*

The lens in the watch face was looking right up at Sal. I looked up at him and grinned. *Yeah, you're right. I must have been off my head, but that's what I did; I grinned up at him.*

He had an insane light in his eyes. He swung the cleaver up and back, and opened his eyes wide. I closed mine, clamped my teeth together, and.... BAM, SMACK.

I was showered with something wet, warm, and sticky. My hands were released. The gun was gone from my neck. BAM. The second shot came before the echo of the first had died away. More wetness. A heavy thud to my left was followed an instant later by another behind me, and I heard the kitchen door fly open.

"Don't move, assholes." Jesus and Tony both raised their hands. "Now step away. You alright, Harry?"

"I am now. Cut it a little close, didn't you?"

Bob grinned. "Had to make sure we had 'em dead to rights, and they both are certainly that, dead. Gazzara is on her way. I called her before I came in. Should be here in a minute."

And she was, along with Lonnie Guest and a half-dozen uniforms.

"Oh my God, Harry," she said, as she ran between the booths. "What the hell have you done?"

"Me? Nothing. They took my weapon. Bob got them. He saved my life. Here." I stripped off the watch and handed it to her. "The recorder is outside in the car. I got it all... I hope." I suddenly had my doubts. *What if the damn thing malfunctioned? Nah! That's CIA equipment.*

294

"Bob," she said, holding out her hand. He handed her his Colt .45.

"Talk to me, Harry," she said, handing the Colt to Lonnie. "You and Bob set him up, didn't you?"

"Kate," I said, trying to sound outraged. "How can you say such a thing?"

"So what the hell happened? Tell me."

"There's not much to tell. I came in alone; came in to talk to De Luca, to try to persuade him to call off his vendetta. I also wanted to ask him about the Dickersons, but I didn't get the chance. He wasn't interested in talking. We'd barely exchanged a couple of words when that one stuck a gun in my ear." I pointed to what was left of Paulie.

"Where the hell he came from I have no idea. They must have been expecting me, I think, after what they did to Jacque. He must have been sitting in one of the booths, in the dark. I was concentrating on De Luca and didn't see him. Anyway, they grabbed me. Sal was going to cut off my hand; almost did." I pointed at the cleaver lying on the floor next to De Luca's right hand. "Bob knew I was coming here. He must have followed me. Whatever, he arrived just in time. If he hadn't, I'd be bleeding to death right now."

She looked down at De Luca, and for the first time, so did I. He was on his back in the doorway;

the self-closing door up against his left side. There was a neat little hole in his face just to the right side of his nose, and a pool of blood around his head. I inwardly shuddered at the thought of what the exit wound must look like: Bob used hollow points.

Paulie was in no better shape. He was on his back in one of the booths. Bob's slug had torn a hole in his neck the size of my fist. He hadn't died quickly; he'd bled out.

It was then that it hit me, with a bang. I looked again at the cleaver. *Goddamn, that was a close call. I've got to quit this silly shit before it kills me. Hell, if Bob had been two steps slower....*

Suddenly, I felt totally washed out, weak at the knees. I had to sit down. I did, on the edge of the bench in one of the booths. I looked again at my right hand, a subconscious check to make sure it was still there.

Kate walked toward the door, her iPhone at her ear. She finished the call and came back; her face was white.

"I have to take you both in. Doc Sheddon and a team are on the way. Damn it, Harry. This time... I dunno. Let's go."

I grinned up at her, nodded, and held out my hands for the cuffs.

"Oh for God's sake, Harry. Get out of here. Lonnie, I'll take Harry. You take Bob; no, you don't need the cuffs."

"What about those two?" Lonnie asked. Jesus and Tony still had their hands in the air.

"Cuff 'em, caution 'em, and charge 'em with attempted murder. You did get them both on the watch, right?" she asked me.

I nodded. *Hell, I hope I did.*

Bob and I were kept separated and were interrogated for the next three hours. Nope, Kate stayed out of it. Where she was, I had no clue, but I figured she was running the recording.

I spent my three hours with Lonnie Guest. *Can you believe that?*

I had badly underestimated Lonnie all these years. He's one hell of an interrogator. He kept at it, over and over, like a dog with a bone. I remember to this day the snide grin he gave me when I turned down his offer to have an attorney present.

Fortunately, Bob and I had it together. We had done nothing illegal.

Yes, we'd set De Luca up, but that's not what we told the cops. My plan had been to provide De Luca with the opportunity to kill me. Bob was supposed to bust in and save the day, just as he had, and everything would be recorded via the watch. What I hadn't planned for was Paulie. It almost came off the rails right there. It was only the fact that Sal had wanted to collect on the perceived debt that saved my ass. Bob and I stuck to our story, that I went in there to try to talk to him and that Bob had decided to follow me, to provide backup, should I need it. Needless to say, no one really believed it, but what the hell. They couldn't prove anything. It worked, and I still had my hand. Lonnie, however, was not convinced.

"Pull the other one, Starke," he said. "You don't negotiate with people who are dedicated to killing you, and you don't walk into a nest of vipers on your own, not unless you're crazy." He grinned, then shook his head. "Then again, maybe you are crazy. Nah, you planned it." He reached out and turned off the machines.

"Nice one, Harry," he said, quietly. It was almost a whisper that only I could hear. "I know what you did, and so does Kate. You got real lucky, and you got away with it... this time."

He was right, of course, but I had no regrets, and eventually Bob and I walked out onto Amnicola, into the last glimmer of the setting sun. It was over.... No. It wasn't, not quite. There was still Brinique.

298

Chapter 35

I spent the next two days trying to figure it out, getting nowhere. I'd gotten into the office early that Saturday morning. Amanda was still staying with me on Lakeshore, and so were Terri and Sandra. To see them now, you wouldn't recognize them. Amanda had hit my American Express card hard, but she'd turned those two little waifs into beautiful kids, and they loved it. It was going to be hard, on all of us, to move them on. Anyway, now that the danger was over, Amanda was back to driving her Lexus, and she'd left the kids at home with Sandra in charge, and gone into the station.

I had two solid suspects, so I thought: the Draycotts. Either he killed the girl as a cover up... of what I had no idea. But that didn't account for the body in the sewer. Second, I kinda liked Doctor Ellen for both. I figured maybe she caught her husband fooling around with Brinique, or Brinique had confronted her about her husband, threatened to expose him, and she killed her to stop it. After all, who was going to miss a homeless kid? If that was what had happened, it also could explain the other body. She would have needed help to put Brinique under the boards. But that would have her exposed to blackmail, or some other kind of pressure from him, thus he ended up in the sewer.

I also figured that the identity of that body was probably Ricky Jessell; as yet we hadn't found him, nor had Tim had any luck with his missing persons search. Samantha had completed the reconstruction several days ago, but the photo of the head hadn't brought in any hits either. The body in the drain was a dead end, literally.

I didn't like either of the Dickersons for it. Hell, I didn't think they even knew Brinique, but I also knew I could have been wrong about that.

And then there was the fact that no one remembered her. None of the inmates we'd interviewed did, and that bothered me a whole lot. I sort of figured that she probably hadn't been at Hill House long enough for people to get to know her; that and the fact that it had been more than ten years ago.

I knew she had to have been there at the time of the transition between the Dickersons and Draycotts. The dates and time of death matched, so did the date of Brinique's disappearance from home, and then of course, she was found under the floorboards.

I figured that we were probably looking at a three to five-week window, from May 27 through the end of June, during which time... well, she died. It couldn't have been any longer than that. If Dickerson really didn't know her, that must put her there either just before or right at the time of the hand over. If he was lying... well, that would really screw things up. Somehow, though, I didn't think he was. *Surely someone would have gotten to know her, remembered her.*

So here's how I broke it down:

May 28: Brinique runs away from home with Ricky Jessell.

May 30: They arrive in Chattanooga. Why? *Now that's a damned good question.*

June 4: Brinique calls home, so she's still alive.

June 20: She's dead and under the boards. Ricky disappears. *It's a guess, but I don't see anything else. The question is, where was she and with whom, from June 4 to June 20?*

That was about all I had: nothing, other than an unfounded suspicion that it was one of the Draycotts. That was it, not a damn thing more. There had to be an answer, probably more than one.

I had the small stack of files on my desk. The ones from the Draycotts; the girls that went missing. Nine of them had disappeared between 2005 and 2008: runaways, probably. I also had the stack of photos in front of me; the ones that Tim had copied from the footage Bob had shot during our first visit. There were fifteen of them, all eight by tens. Some were in color, some were black and white. Almost all of them slightly blurred or out of focus, probably due to the way Bob had shot them. Still, the people in them were, for the most part, recognizable. I shuffled through the stack of photos, not really knowing what I was looking for, hoping something would grab my attention. It didn't. I directed my attention to those taken during the transition from the Dickersons to the Draycotts.

I had a magnifying glass, but it didn't help much. The photos were old, and the watch was not the best instrument for making copies. In some cases, the magnifying glass made it a whole lot worse: those fuzzy images turned into a hazy, unrecognizable mess.

One by one, I sifted through them, discarded some, and placed others in a pile to be looked at again. When I'd finished, I'd reduced the stack to just four that were of particular interest: the group photos taken during the time when the Draycotts were at Hill House. All had been taken at the same time, on the rear steps, rear porch, and balcony of the house

All of them included both the Dickersons and the Draycotts. Three also included what I assumed must be the inmates, more than twenty of them: some on the balcony, some on the porch. The fourth photo was the one that included only the four principles: Sam Draycott had his arm around Billy

Dickerson's shoulder; Ellen Draycott was standing next to Billy; India was next to Sam.

The features of the people in the three group photos were difficult to distinguish. The images had been shot from a distance with negative film and then printed. The viewpoint was from somewhere left of the stone steps, now long gone. The people were small, the faces smaller still. Some of the people were in all three photos, some only in one.

I stared at each one through the glass until my eyes hurt. I discarded two more, including the one with just the Draycotts and Dickersons. Hell, I knew who they were, for God's sake.

Now I was left with just two images, both group shots. I went out, got a cup of coffee, and sat down again. I put the two photos side by side in front of me and sipped on the hot beverage as I stared down at them. I thought I recognized one of those people at the back of the group on the porch. He was also there on the second image, but half hidden by the person in front of him. I wasn't absolutely sure, but it looked like a young Darius Willett. He was standing next to a girl, but the quality of the print was too poor to make out the features; still... it could be.

I opened the desk drawer and withdrew the images of Brinique that the Williams had left with me. I looked back and forth, from the group photos to those of Brinique. The hairstyle looked the same, but.... Finally, I leaned back in my chair and threw the glass down on the desk. It was no good. The images were too bad. My head was throbbing. I'd had enough. I needed to see the originals.

I was about to get up and go for another coffee, when something stirred in the back of my brain. It was to do with the files, the nine files for the missing girls. I flipped through them quickly. Nothing, and then the obvious hit me. These girls had all gone missing. If Brinique *had* been there, then she *hadn't* gone missing. If she had, there would have been a file for her. It was either that or her file had been removed, which was of course, an option. Still....

And there was something else. It had been niggling at me for the last hour, but I couldn't put my finger on what it was.

I grabbed the magnifying glass and began to scrutinize the group photos again. *Come on, Harry. It must be staring you in the damned face.*

And it was, but I still didn't spot it, not until I put the glass down and leaned back in my chair. It was then I spotted the image of the principles. I'd shoved it all the way over to the right side of my desk, behind the phone, so that I could spread the rest of the photos out across the desk top.

I picked it up, and the glass, and studied it. Nothing. *Whoa, Harry, what's that?*

What it was... was a necklace Doctor Ellen was wearing. It was a cross on a thin chain, the same one the corpse had been wearing. *Hah.... Okay, so now what? What the hell does it mean? It means we need to see the original, dumb ass. Could she have given it to the kid? Is she a? Nah! Then what?*

I couldn't figure it out, but I knew I was right. I needed to make sure; I needed to see the original images, and better yet, I needed to re-interview the Draycotts, both of them, but especially Ellen. That, I knew, would not be well received. *Hmmm*

I thought about calling Kate, then I thought I wouldn't. Then I changed my mind again. If there was something going on, I would need official backup. I made the call.

"Hey, Kate. You busy?"

"I'm always busy, Harry. You know that. What do you need?"

"We need to talk. We need to go see the Draycotts again. Where are you?"

"I'm in my office. Harry, I don't know about this. They were kinda pissed the last time, when we hauled off all of their files. You sure this is necessary?"

"Yeah. There are a couple of things. One is I need to see those images on the reception wall. ... Yeah.... yeah, I know I already have them, but they are no good. The quality is very poor. And there's something else. Can you bring that cross and chain with you?"

I explained why, and she agreed. I would meet her at the Draycotts' place in an hour, but first she insisted on calling them to tell them we were on the way. I didn't like that worth a damn, but I could see her point. If she was to be involved, she needed to cover her ass. She did, however, agree to be vague about why we needed to see them. We sure as hell didn't want anything removed before we got there.

Kate was already inside the compound when I arrived. I talked nicely to the little electronic box, and the gate rolled open. And then I was struck by that, too. Security is one thing, but wasn't this a little over the top? They were not, after all, running a prison, or were they?

Kate was on her own. Where she'd left Lonnie, I had no idea, and I didn't ask. Together, we walked through the glass doors into the lobby, where Doctor Ellen Draycott was waiting for us.

"Where's your husband, ma'am?" Kate asked, without preamble. "We'd like to see him, too."

"And good afternoon to you, too, Lieutenant, and to you, Mr. Starke." The sarcasm was palpable, and she was, as I had expected, angry enough to bite a sixpenny nail in two.

"Thank you for agreeing to see us, Doctor," I said, as I walked past her to the wall where the photographs were hanging. "I need to take a look at some of these photos, if you don't mind." I began to take them down from the wall.

I removed the three that I'd studied back in my office and set them side by side on the reception desk, took my glass from my coat pocket, and again studied the image with the four principles. *Yup. That's it. That's the cross.*

"Lieutenant," I said. "The cross. Would you mind showing it to her, please?"

Kate withdrew a small, clear plastic evidence envelope from her pocket and handed it to her.

"That belongs to you, does it not?" I asked. "You're wearing it in this photograph taken during the transition. What I want to know is, how did Brinique Williams come to be wearing it when she died?"

She looked at it, smiled, and handed it back. She didn't look at all perturbed. "If you would wait here for a moment, I think I can explain." She walked out of the lobby and then returned a few moments later.

"Here," she said, holding out her hand. "This is the cross I was wearing in the photograph and, as I told you before, I do not, did not, know Brinique Williams."

I looked at the cross, then picked up my glass and looked again at the photo. No doubt about it, they were the same. I held out my hand to Kate. She handed me the envelope. They were similar, almost identical, about the same size, but the doctor's was of a slightly different design. *Damn! Damn! Damn!*

"I'm sorry, Doctor," I said. "I really am. I don't know what else to say. Please forgive me."

"It's all right, Mr. Starke. I can understand how you could mistake that one for mine. No harm done, I think."

"Thank you, ma'am." I handed hers back to her and the envelope back to Kate.

"If you don't mind," I said. "I have a couple more questions, about these two group photos."

She looked puzzled, but slowly nodded. "Of course. If I can."

"Thank you. Please look at this one. It was taken the day you and Dr. Draycott took over from the Dickersons, June 20, I believe. This is Brinique, I think. Do you recognize her?" I pointed to the figure at the back of the group.

308

She took the glass from me and, for a long moment, she stared through it at the image. Finally, she looked up and shook her head. "No, I've never seen her before." She offered the glass to me.

"Just one more look, please, Doctor. The boy standing next to her, to her right, that's Darius Willett, right? That one there." I pointed him out to her.

Again, she stared at the photo.

"That's Darius Willett," she said, pushing the photo toward me, pointing.

I smiled, looked at Kate, and nodded. Then I looked at the doctor. She was still pointing. Her finger was touching the glass. She wasn't smiling. I looked again.

"No," I said. "I mean this boy, here."

"And I said that this is Darius Willett." She was pointing at the smiling boy to Brinique's *left*.

I looked at the boy, then at her, then at the boy again. "Are you sure?"

"I'm certain. I've never seen the other boy before."

"Then who the hell is he?" I was shocked out of my brains, and so, by the look on her face, was Kate.

"I don't know," the doctor said, "but it's not Darius Willett. That's him, and he left that day along

309

with the Dickersons and several more of the people that had been with him for some time. I've not seen him since. Oh, there you are, Sam. Come here and look at these photos, will you?"

"Hello, you two," Sam Draycott said. "Ellen said you were coming. What can I do for you?"

"Please, if you wouldn't mind, Doctor," I said. "Point out Darius Willett in this photo."

"All right. If I can.... Yes, that's him, there." He pointed. He didn't even need the glass. He picked out the same kid Ellen had. *What the f...? If that's Willett, who the hell is* he?

I stood, staring down at the photo, feeling stupid. Two huge mistakes in the space of just a few minutes. Then it came to me, and I looked up and grinned.

"What, Harry?" Kate said.

"I'm not sure, but I have an idea. I'll tell you later. In the meantime, Doctors, I want first to apologize to you both for being a pain in the ass and... well, I'm sorry. I hope you'll forgive me."

They both nodded. "Of course. You were just doing your job, even if.... Well, it doesn't matter." Ellen even smiled at me as she said it. She was actually quite attractive. "What else was it, Mr. Starke?"

"Lieutenant Gazzara arrested the Dickersons yesterday and charged them with a whole litany of felonies, including trafficking."

"Yes, we heard," Doctor Sam said. "It was on the news this morning. How does that affect us?"

"Well... it doesn't except that.... I have two of his kids staying with me. They're good kids, victims. They need a home, and all sorts of help: medical, psychological, practical, the sort of help you specialize in here. I was wondering...."

"Yes, of course," Ellen said. "Bring them by. We'll interview them and... well, we'll see."

"Look," I said. "If it's money. I can handle that. I just can't keep them with me. You guys can do them a lot of good. I'll pay their way."

"You don't have to do that, Mr. Starke," Sam said, with a smile. "Although donations are always welcome. I'm sure we can work something out. When can you bring them in?"

I made arrangements for Monday afternoon, the 11th, thanked them for their understanding, asked for permission to borrow the photographs, and we left.

"What the hell was all that stuff about Willett?" Kate asked, as we walked back to the cars.

"You'll see," I said. "Let's go talk to him."

Chapter 36

Darius was waiting for us when we arrived. He was seated at the table in the interview room, dressed in an orange jumpsuit, a Coke in one hand, tapping the tabletop with the fingers of the other. He was smiling, but he looked a little chastened.

"What you want now?" he asked as Kate and I sat down opposite him.

Kate looked at me. "It's your party, Harry. Have at it."

"Better caution him first," I said.

She did. She turned on the equipment, identified those present, and asked him again if he would like an attorney present.

He looked puzzled. "Whaaat?"

"Ricky," I said. "I really think you need your attorney."

"Whaaat?" he repeated, his face screwed up. "What Ricky?"

"Oh come on," I said, pleasantly. "It's over. I know who you really are. Here look." I pushed the photo across the table so that he could see it.

"That's you, there. That's Brinique Williams and that's Darius Willett. You want to tell me about it?"

"You wrong, man. It t'other way roun'."

"Give it up, Ricky. Both Draycotts identified you, and I know damned well the Dickersons will give you up in exchange for a plea. Now tell us. What happened to Darius, and what the hell happened to Brinique Williams?"

He picked up the photograph, stared at it for a few moments, then smiled. "She fine. Sweet little thing. I screwed that little girl good, on'y she din't want to, least not that day, but befo', oh yeah. She screamed, man; hit me in the face wit' a board; ran. She hurt me, man. She a bitch. I grabbed her, slapped her silly, took off her threads...." He paused for a moment, smiling, then continued.

"Oh she was fine: skinny fine, smooth.... and then in walks that little shit Willett. He saw what we was doin' an' he ran. She was screamin' again, man. I din't know what to do. I grabbed her, an', an', an she stopped screamin'. Tha's it. Din't mean to...."

H stared down at the photograph, breathing slowly through his open mouth.

"Then what, Ricky?" I asked.

He shrugged. "She daid, man. I din't know what to do. Then I saw the boards was loose. Electricians had been doin' somthin'. I took one up, grabbed some plastic stuff in the corner, wrapped 'er up, an' put 'er under. Came back later and nailed it down. Tha's it, man."

313

"What about Darius?"

"Hah, that li'l shit. I foun' 'im in the basement. Smacked him in the head wit' a rock, tipped 'im head fust down the hole, an' put the lid on. Easy. Then I took his stuff and got outa there. Went after Billy an' asked 'im for a job. He gimme one; bin wid 'im ever since. Cool huh? Tha's it; tha's all."

"Was he dead, when you put him into the sewer?"

"Hell, man. How I know that?"

I couldn't believe what I was hearing. He was one cold-blooded son of a bitch. I didn't want to look at him anymore, but I had to get the rest of it, while he was talking.

"And you just took his identity?"

"Yeah. It was easy, man. I jus' took 'is stuff, 'is bill fol', an' that. He dint have no license, just a social card. Hell, man it was 'is birfday that day I put 'im down the drain. I jus' went down the DMV and got me a driver's license. Tha's it. I was Darius."

"Brinique; you met her in Greenville, right?" I asked.

"Tha's right. Tha's where we lived, both of us, but I'd heerd about Billy an' was after workin' for 'im. I figured I could get them ladies for 'im; always could. I heered about 'im on the web, the Dark Web. He damn famous there. I met her at the mall, dated

314

her fo' a while, maybe a couple months, made it with 'er, tol' 'er we'd go south, start a new life, be together, always. She b'lieved me... at first. Then that night I told 'er I was taking her.... Well, she din't want that, did she?"

"Ricky Jessell?" Kate said.

"Name's Richard," he interrupted, grinning at her across the table.

"Richard Jessell...." She cautioned him again, and then charged him with the second-degree murder of Brinique Williams and the first-degree murder of Darius Willett. I just sat there and listened, my imagination running wild. Then I got up and got out of there. I had to.

Chapter 37

The following Monday morning, the 11th, I got some good news: Jacque was to be released from the hospital the next day, but was going to be laid up for several weeks. Lucy would take care of her.

Amanda and I delivered the two girls to the Draycotts that afternoon as arranged. They weren't too sure about it, but when they met Doctor Sam and learned they wouldn't be separated, they accepted it for what it was. Both of them, young as they were, were worldly wise, and recognized that they were being offered a chance of a better life, and they embraced it.

Amanda had set them up with everything they would need in the short term, clothes, toiletries, whatever. I assured them and Sam Draycott that I would look after their future needs, at least until they became self-sufficient.

Parting from them wasn't easy. Amanda, even though she had been with them just a few short days, had grown attached to them, and so had I. There were hugs, tears, more hugs, more tears, and we left them. We both promised to drop by often and see them.

That wasn't the only parting I had to cope with that day. Amanda decided that enough was enough and she moved back into her apartment. I wasn't too sure if I was happy about that, but I soon settled back into my old routine. It was good to get my life back, although....

Two days after I'd parted from the kids, and Amanda had moved out, I had Kate over for dinner. It was just a casual thing: nice food, a couple of drinks, and a few quiet moments. We talked about the case, but not much. We'd both had enough of that, and that was it. She left before eleven that night, gave me a peck on the cheek, and was gone.

The great river was calm that night, a vast, flat expanse of blackness highlighted by the reflections of the lights on the Thrasher Bridge. I was calm, too. I sat for an hour, thinking about the turbulent events of the past year: Tabitha Willard, Charlie Maxwell, Tom Sattler, Brinique, Terri and Sandra, Sal De Luca, Kate, and... Amanda, always Amanda.

Finally, I dragged myself together, got up from the sofa, walked to the window, stood for a moment, and.... *It's time to move on, Harry. Time to turn the page.*

Thank you.

I hope you enjoyed reading this story as much as I did writing it. If you did, I really would appreciate it if you would take just a minute to write a brief review on Amazon (just a sentence will do).

Reviews are so very important. I don't have the backing of a major New York publisher. I can't afford take out ads in the newspapers and on TV, but you can help get the word out. I would be very grateful if you would spend just a couple of minutes and leave a review. You can jump to the page by clicking the links below.

If you have comments or questions, you can contact me by email at blair@blairhoward.com, and you can visit my website http://www.blairhoward.com.

This was book 3 in the series. If you haven't already read them, you may also enjoy reading the other Harry Starke novels. They are all stand-alone stories: no cliff hangers,

Harry Starke – Book 1

It's almost midnight, bitterly cold, snowing, when a beautiful young girl, Tabitha Willard, throws herself off the Walnut Street Bridge into the icy waters of the Tennessee. Harry Starke is there, on the bridge. Wrong time, wrong place? Maybe. He tries, but is unable to stop her. Thus begins a series of events and an investigation that involves a local United States congressman, a senior lady senator from Boston, a local crime boss, several very nasty individuals, sex, extortion, high finance, corruption, and three murders. Harry has to work his way through a web of deceit and corruption until finally.... Well, as always, there's a twist in the tale, several in fact.

You can grab your copy here:

Amazon U.S. http://amzn.to/1K8zCrl

Amazon U.K. http://amzn.to/1RUx5XW

If you're a Kindle Unlimited member, you can read it for free.

Two for the Money – Harry Starke Book 2

Who Killed Tom Sattler? Who Stole $350 Million from New Vision Strategic Investments?

It's up to Harry Starke to Figure it out

The call came on a Tuesday evening in the middle of August at around nine-thirty. It was from an old school friend that Harry Starke hadn't heard from in almost five years, and he hadn't thought about him in almost as long. Tom Sattler wanted to meet with Harry urgently, and it wouldn't wait until morning. When Harry arrived at Sattler's luxury home less than an hour later, he found him dead, lying in a pool of blood, a single gunshot wound to the head, and .22 revolver lying close to his hand.

Suicide? If he was going to do that, why the hell did he call me?

The search for an answer to that question starts Harry on wide ranging investigation that involves murder, corruption, organized crime, and, deception.

You can grab your copy here:

Amazon U.S. and here's the actual link: http://amzn.to/1MRsdmo

Amazon U.K. or http://amzn.to/1KlQk6n

As always, if you're a Kindle Unlimited member, you can read it for free.